Rampage

Iron Hammers MC

Khloe Wren

Cover Credits:

Models: Kristen Laz-Wood & Charlie Smith

Photographer: JW Photography

Digital Artist: Khloe Wren

Editor: Carolyn Deprew of Write Right Edits

Proofreader: Kelly Klau

Chapter One

Timber Cove, Sonoma County, California

Cujo

Considering how much I hated fucking cages or cells of any kind, I probably should have chosen a different profession. But there weren't a lot of employment options for a mostly feral wolf shifter like me. Over the years, I'd built up a good reputation for being able to do *anything* a client needed. Some called me a mercenary, some a gun for hire. Basically, I was whatever the customer needed. I didn't mind getting my hands dirty and wasn't constrained by any sort of fucking moral code. My only rule: no kids.

From where I sat in the back of local Sheriff Jaxson's SUV, I looked through the plexiglass partition and windshield to the landscape passing us by while I tried to stay calm. Tried to keep my wolf from going batshit crazy at being locked in here. While the interior of the vehicle wasn't overly cramped, both my wolf and I knew we were heading to lock-up, where we'd end up in a damn cell. The steel cuffs that dug into my wrists reminded me of my past. Of other times when I'd been restrained, something that had my wolf clawing at my insides to get out and save us.

When I licked my lips, I tasted the salt from my sweat. I wasn't going to last much longer before my wolf ripped free and all hell would break loose. While these steel cuffs would probably hold a normal shifter, if my animal went into a rage, they wouldn't slow me down much. The joys of having been experimented on for most of my childhood meant there wasn't much about me that could be classified as normal.

Jaxson frowned into the mirror at me. "Are you able to hold off your shift? If not, I can give you something that'll help."

My acute shifter hearing picked up his voice through the plexiglass without any issue and my entire body jolted at the mention of drugs. That was an even bigger fucking trigger for me than cages were.

"No fucking drugs. I'll hold my beast. He doesn't like being caged."

Jaxson continued to watch me in the mirror. "Lock-up's going to be fun for you, then."

I jerked my head in a nod. "Won't end well. There any way we can avoid me being put in a cell?"

The growl I got in response let me know Jaxson was still pissed off over what had happened and wasn't going to do me any favors.

"You kidnapped a female shifter for the purpose of putting her up for a Trial. You're going to do time, asshole."

Considering Alina was sitting right fucking next to him, safe and sound, I wasn't sure why he was so angry. Hell, I'd given him an excuse to play the white knight who had to come riding to her rescue. I'd fucking helped him from my perspective, but I wasn't stupid enough to say that out loud to the man. I stilled as I did think of something I could say to maybe help him decide to cut me some slack. "A Trial you were there to partake in, weren't you, Deputy?"

Putting an unmated, fertile female wolf shifter through a Trial to be mated off to the winning male shifter was an ancient tradition. One that had been deemed illegal some time ago.

Alina jerked in her seat as though she'd been struck before she glared at Jaxson.

"You were going to— Why would you do that?"

Jaxson's focus shifted back to the road, his body going rigid. "I can explain, Alina, but not now. Not here."

Alina had told me how she didn't like games, and it looked like the not-so-good-deputy was playing a big one with the little wolf. I held in a smirk as I remembered how feisty Alina could get. Jaxson had a hell of a lot of explaining to do to his mate. Hopefully he wanted to do that more than he wanted to process all the paperwork required to lock me away.

"I don't have the name of the fucker who hired me, but what if I gave you his phone number and bank account details? Would that buy me some damn leniency? I mean, I personally didn't put her on fucking Trial. My job was to snatch her and transport her to a location. How the fuck was I to know it was for an old-school Trial?"

Alina spun to glare at me. "You liar. You knew. You came to me to tell me that I had to go in the stupid Trial to earn my freedom!"

I raised an eyebrow. "Who's to say I knew any fucking thing about that before I delivered you to the cabin?"

Jaxson's growl cut off any response Alina might have given me.

"Enough!" Jaxson barked. "If you give me everything you have on who hired you, and *if* it checks out, I'll look at downgrading the charges to something that won't have you doing time." He paused until I looked into the mirror, locking my gaze with his. "But I'll only do that if I can release you into the custody of your Alpha. I want you far away from my territory as soon as possible, and I want your Alpha's guarantee that you'll stay away."

Aw, fuck. Was he trying to trick me? Force me to accept jail time? Surely, he could guess a wolf like me didn't have a damn pack. I hadn't since I was stolen as a cub. Not even sure I'd know how to be part of a fucking pack, but this was going to be my only chance to not have to spend the next few years in a fucking cage. If I lasted that long. If my wolf got loose and went crazy, they'd most likely have to put me down. It'd be the only way to stop the rampage he'd go on.

Looking down at my worn boots, I wracked my brain for who I could call on. I'd done jobs for several wolf shifter packs over the years, but most of the Alphas weren't the type to tolerate a rogue feral like me. Then I remembered a shifter I'd come across in the south of Texas a while back. He'd hired me to do some investigative work to search for a missing female shifter. Joaquin was the Alpha and president of the Iron Hammers MC. His crew was a mixed bag of all sorts of shifters. He might take me on for however long Jaxson was going to stipulate. It'd probably cost me more than just money, but if it kept me out of a cell, it'd be worth it.

"Time's ticking."

Jaxson growled the words like he was looking forward to me not being able to come up with a name. Fuck him. "Joaquin Torres. He's Alpha and president of the Iron Hammers MC over in Galveston, Texas. Let me give him a call. I promise to leave with him and never return."

He narrowed his gaze at me in the mirror again, and I started to panic he was going to change his mind and back out of the deal. But before he could say anything, Alina reached over and wrapped her palm around his forearm, gaining his full attention.

"Please, Jaxson," Alina begged. "The last thing my babies or I need is for it to get out that I was kidnapped and put up for Trial. That kind of thing would forever tarnish my reputation and could cause issues for the twins when they're older. They already have a nightmare hanging over their head due to their father. I can't take dealing with another mess. Please, just take me to wherever my babies are, then you can take him in, get whatever information he has and let him go before coming back to join me."

The emotion in her voice was clear for anyone to hear, and hopefully it would help sway Jaxson in my favor.

He smacked a hand against the steering wheel as he growled low and muttered something under his breath.

"Fine. But, Cujo, you're in lock-up until I can check out your information and get this Joaquin up here to collect your ass. I won't have you roaming my territory unsupervised. And I'll be calling him, not you."

With a quick nod I sat back, trying to relax. A short time in lock-up. I hoped I could hold it together that long.

Hoped Joaquin would not only remember who the fuck I was, but would agree to take me in. Fuck, I hated when I had to rely on others for anything, especially when the stakes were this high. I much preferred to have to only rely on myself. After all, I was the only one I could fucking trust to not screw me over.

· · · • • • • • · · ·

Lily-Rose

A loud bang had me jolting to attention. Surely my piece of shit father hadn't come to bail me out already? Normally, he'd make me wait at least until the next morning. Moron thought it was making me suffer by leaving me here. Little did he know, I preferred a night in here to the alternative of being out in the world where he controlled every aspect of my life.

I hoped he never found out because he delighted in taking whatever it was away from me and crushing all of my dreams. Long ago, I learned to keep everything tightly locked down.

Deputy Jaxson Salvador entering the cell block before morning wouldn't ordinarily have me coming to full attention, except the large wolf shifter was struggling to drag a man who had to be as big, if not bigger than him, into the cell next to mine. As soon as the deputy swung the man around so he faced me, our gazes locked and everything in me stilled. His eyes were unlike anything I'd ever seen before—ice blue with silver threads through the blue. The instant effect he had on me was as shocking as the time I'd snuck away and gone night swimming at the beach and a huge wave had come out of nowhere and crashed over me. Just like that night, this stranger's mere presence took my breath away with a gasp.

He'd also stilled when our gazes clashed, and that allowed the deputy to finally wrangle him inside the cell. The clank of the door shutting had his eyes widening before he spun toward the sound. His skin rippled, revealing he was a shifter and was not coping well with being confined. By the time he slammed against the locked door, he was a giant wolf, larger than any other wolf shifter I'd ever seen. With a growl that had the hair on my body standing up, he continued to slam his huge form against the bars, rattling everything near him.

My own inner animal, an ocelot, wanted to reach out to him, to soothe the beast, but my self-preservation instincts were stronger than my ocelot's need to calm whoever this guy was.

"Fuck. Guess you weren't exaggerating what would happen, huh?" With a shake of his head, the deputy reached up to the wall and grabbed a tranq gun that sat there for just this situation. Without any hesitation, he pointed and shot two darts into the wolf, who was still going crazy trying to knock out the bars.

The deputy ignored the wolf and turned his focus to me. All the officers here were nice to me. They knew who held my leash and that he forced me into the prostitution that got me occasionally arrested. I think they'd worked out that I preferred a night here to out on the street, even if it got me a beating the next day in payment for screwing up and costing him money – both in lost revenue and the fine he'd have to pay to cut me loose. This deputy in particular, Jaxson Salvador, was a good man. Part of the Timber Cove Wolves MC, he was also a wolf shifter. His family ran the motorcycle shop here in town and early on, he'd tried to convince me to choose a different path for my life. Not that I ever had a choice in the matter. But I appreciated the gesture all the same.

"That should keep him out till at least morning. We'll keep an eye on the cameras to make sure he doesn't do anything that could endanger you."

I nodded but stayed curled up on the far side of my cell, far away from the stranger who'd morphed from watching me calmly to a rampaging beast in seconds. They could tell me he was going to stay out cold all they liked, but I was still going to be cautious all the same. "Thanks, Deputy."

With a small smile, he turned and left me alone with the beast. At the sound of my voice, the wolf turned from the door and staggered over toward the bars that separated our cells. He was obviously having trouble focusing as his gaze scanned my cell, searching for me. Just as he located me, his big body crashed to the floor and he let out a pitiful sounding whine. His tongue hung out the side of his mouth, making him almost appear friendly. The silver threaded through his ice blue irises was glowing now and they held me mesmerized as he watched me for a few moments before with another whine, his lids closed and his entire body relaxed into unconsciousness.

Lifting my right hand, I started chewing on the nail of my middle finger. It was a nervous habit I'd never been able to kick, and one that drove my father crazy because apparently my torn-up nails made me less marketable. I rolled my eyes at that thought. Like the Johns I was forced to entertain gave a fuck about my nails. They cared if I could fuck, that was all. Sure, most of them appreciated my long, white-blonde hair and my clear, steel-blue irises that were ringed in black. They certainly appreciated my agility and abilities... but not one of them had ever commented on my short nails or ragged skin around the cuticles from where I'd bitten at them constantly.

"Go to him. He needs us."

Seemed like my ocelot had taken a liking to this beast of a shifter.

"He could hurt us," I murmured back to her.

My cat shook her head. *"He'll protect us. He's ours."*

She'd lost her damn mind. Why on earth would this stranger want to protect me? He seemed rather feral and maybe even deranged. After waiting a few minutes to be sure he was going to stay knocked out, I began to move from my position. Slowly, I crept across the cell toward where he was laying close to the bars. Thanks to the stupid, magic-infused leather bracelets my father had locked onto both my wrists, I couldn't shift, but my ocelot was still within me, gifting me with her heightened senses.

Crouching down to get close to him, I inhaled and froze when, purring, my ocelot shook out her spotted coat before rolling over to expose her belly. What the hell was wrong with her? Tentatively, I reached through the bars and with a single finger, touched his fur. Sparks flew up my arm and I snatched my hand back. That reaction was definitely both unfamiliar and unexpected, but it hadn't been entirely unpleasant.

After rubbing my arm to dispel the sparks, I moved to sit on the concrete near him. Something deep inside me wouldn't allow me to pull away now that I was close. Was this a shifter thing? My mother was the only shifter I'd known well enough to ask questions, but she'd never spoken to me about our animal side. My asshole father had put the magical bracelets on her too, restricting both of us from being able to shift. The way my mother, Mary-Lou, chose to deal with it was to pretend that side of her didn't exist, but I loved my ocelot. She was often my only friend and comfort, especially after Mom was gone. I hated how sad she became that she couldn't come out and run free, but since I'd only ever shifted the one time when I was young, I barely remembered what it was like. I hoped she couldn't remember either. That it made it easier for her to bear being stuck within my human body all the time.

"Touch him. Connect us."

"Why?" I whispered the word, not wanting to risk disturbing the wolf.

"He's our mate. We are meant to be connected."

"Mate? Oh, hell no."

"Oh, yes. He will free us. Keep us safe."

She pranced around in a circle in my mind, her ears up and tail swishing in excitement, even as my heart began to pound within my chest. My human side did not share my cat's enthusiasm. Nope, that part was freaking the fuck out. A mate? I knew nothing about what that meant. And he was huge, both as a man and wolf. He could crush me with barely a thought. This couldn't be good.

Tears sprang to my eyes, and I buried my face in my hands to hide them from the world. Wasn't my life already difficult enough? I didn't need yet another man who'd think he owned me and could order me around.

Chapter Two

Cujo

Sounds of the night greeted me when I regained consciousness. What the hell had happened? My head throbbed like someone was pounding on my skull with a hammer. From the fucking inside. I inhaled deeply and a fresh scent filled my lungs, easing the pain in my head instantly. Needing more relief before I tried to open my eyes, I took another deep breath. The essence was floral. Honeysuckle, maybe. After a third breath of the intoxicating scent, I forced my eyes to open only to discover I was lying in my wolf form on the concrete floor of a cell.

What the fuck?

Memories of the previous night came back to me. Of Jaxson shoving me in here then tranqing me when I'd lost my shit. I braced myself for my wolf to take over again and rush the bars like he'd done last night. When after a few minutes he hadn't even attempted to move, curiosity had me lifting my head to find who, or what, was putting off the scent that was taming my wolf. A small blonde woman was curled up on the floor of the cell next to mine. There was a cot against the opposite wall, so her choice to sleep near me on the cold concrete was beyond strange. I was certain I'd never met or even seen her before last night. In her sleep, the woman's hand had shifted to lay close to the bars. Shuffling forward, I pressed my snout through so I could sniff right up against her skin. Tingles ran down my spine as the honeysuckle aroma grew thicker and filled my lungs.

"Mate."

Whoa. What the fuck?

I forced myself to back away from the female, shaking my head at what my wolf was telling me. She couldn't possibly be my mate. I'd scented no wolf on her. No shifter at all. No way could I be paired with a fucking human. Fate wouldn't be so cruel as to tie me down to someone as fragile as this woman appeared to be. She was wearing a tight, short skirt and her top barely covered her lush tits. She'd clearly been wearing a lot of makeup and it had smudged since she'd been here, not that it hid her beauty. Her feet were bare, but I could see a pair of high, pointy, heeled shoes over by the cot. She was a hooker. My mate was a fucking prostitute? A low growl rumbled from my chest. Yeah, my wolf also was not impressed at the thought my mate earned money by fucking other men.

I wanted to laugh or maybe cry. Fate was indeed a cruel bitch to pull this shit on me. At least as a human, she wouldn't know we were mates. She'd move on with her life without giving me another thought. No mate meant no family for me, but I didn't need or fucking want either of those, so this was all fine. My wolf growled again and pushing aside my human element, moved over to the bars again where he laid down pressed up against them, trying to get as close to her as he could.

"Mate. Needs rest."

Fucking wolf. Clearly, he didn't agree with my plan to remain single. This was going to be one hell of a mess to sort through, but it wasn't anything I could deal with now. Not only was my wolf refusing to allow me to shift back to human, he was set on letting her continue to sleep. Since it was early morning from what I could sense, there were hours left before the sun would rise, and even longer before Joaquin would be able to make it here from Texas. Assuming he agreed to even come.

My wolf huffed at me, then put his snout through the bars to rest against her palm, settling in to sleep himself. Stubborn animal wasn't taking any suggestions from my human side, but since he also wasn't trying to break out of the cell or anything else that would have us getting tranqed again, I took it as a win for now and allowed sleep to take me away surrounded by the sweet scent of my mate.

The next time I woke it was because she was trying to slide her palm out from beneath my snout. Lifting my head, I blinked my vision clear to take in what this woman looked like in the morning light.

"Mate."

Wish my wolf would cut that shit out. For real. The last complication my life needed right now was a mate. Especially one who fucking sold her body to other males. That had a low growl coming from my wolf and that sent the little female skittering away from me to the other side of her cell.

"I just needed to move off the cold floor. I wasn't going to hurt you or anything."

That had me scoffing. As if she could hurt me. Standing up, I stretched out my body before shaking out my coat. I wished I could get out of this place, but at least my wolf was calm. Which was strange enough to have me reassessing this female as a potential mate.

"Um, do you think you could shift? So we can talk."

Interesting. Why would she want to talk to me if she didn't know we were mates? Now that she'd asked my wolf to hand the reins over, he reluctantly did so. Calling on the magic needed to shift, I stretched up into my human form. When I could see clearly again, she was watching me, mesmerized.

"Damn, I wish I could do that."

I cocked my head at her quietly spoken words. "You wish you were a shifter?"

She frowned and lifting her hand, began to chew on her right index fingernail as she wrapped the other arm around her middle. There was a thick band around each of her wrists. They looked to be made of simple leather, but they had symbols burned into the hide and when I focused on them, I could sense they contained magic.

I shook my head. "No, that's not it. You are a shifter, but you can't shift for some reason. Is it the bracelets?"

She stilled and her eyes widened to let me know I'd hit the mark. If she were a shifter, there was hope she could handle being my mate after all. Even after just the short time we'd been close to each other, I was already becoming addicted to her scent and the effect it had on me. I moved closer, wrapping my hands around the bars. A blast of her fear hit me, and I winced.

"I mean you no harm, sweetheart. What's your name?"

She tilted her head up to look into my gaze. "Lily-Rose. What's yours?"

"I'm Cujo. I can't scent your animal."

With a frown, she started to reach for one of the bands but pulled away before she came into contact with it, although it was enough to confirm it was the bracelets that were limiting her magic. Normally I didn't like to talk, preferring silence, but I needed to know enough about this little female so I could find her later. Even if it meant breaking my promise to Jaxson about leaving the area right away.

· · · • • · • • • · ·

Lily-Rose

This man was way too intuitive. I'd hardly spoken to him and he'd already figured out my biggest secrets. It was disconcerting to have him know about the bracelets, and now he obviously wanted me to tell him what my animal was. But I barely knew him and had no idea if I could trust him. Just because my ocelot was on board with this whole mate thing didn't mean my human side was ready to simply accept it, no questions asked.

I didn't move my gaze from him as I stayed on the opposite side of the cell, chewing my fingernail while I took him in. He was deteriorating, but I wasn't sure why or what was wrong with him. His knuckles were now white where he gripped the bars tightly, and even from here I could see the sweat beading on his skin, which had paled considerably in the past few minutes.

"Are you okay?"

He squeezed his eyes closed for a moment as his face screwed up into a wince. With a deep breath, his lids lifted and he and stared straight at me, drawing me in with those unique irises of his.

"Could you come closer? It's better when you're near me."

I gulped before licking my lips. "What's better? I don't understand."

He winced again, as if it were painful to share whatever it was he was contemplating telling me. "I don't do well in cages of any sort. You saw what happened last night. That will happen again if I can't get my wolf to calm down. With you close earlier, he remained calm in this cell. So, could you please just stand a little closer? I mean you no harm, I just want a little peace."

Emotion welled up, clogging my throat. To have such am adverse physical reaction to cages, one that he couldn't seem to help, most likely meant he'd been forced to live in one at some point in his life. Considering how big and strong he was now, I would guess it had happened when he was younger. Smaller.

Sticking to the outside of the cell, I made my way around to where he was standing. The closer I got, the more settled I felt too. It was strange the way my mind calmed around him. I stayed just out of what I judged to be his reach, hoping that would be close enough, and leaned against the cold metal bars.

He rested his head against the iron, taking deep breaths as his body relaxed. His knuckles weren't white anymore and his skin was a better color now. After a few minutes, he turned to hold my gaze with his again.

"Where do you live? I need to be able to find you after we're out of here."

Panic shot through my system as I shook my head. "No, he'll kill you. You can't—"

Faster than I could track, he was next to me, reaching through the bars to cup my face in his palms. On autopilot, I lifted my hands to wrap my fingers around his wrists, but I didn't try to pull away. The tingles racing over my skin were distracting, however nothing could pull my gaze from his hypnotic one. Not when he was this close. His scent, a mix of pine and sea spray, filled my lungs.

His voice was a low growl, demanding my compliance. "Who the fuck is this man? Is he the one who controls you with the bracelets?"

I didn't want to answer, didn't want to utter his name, but I couldn't resist Cujo's commanding tone. "Kevin Evans. He's my father and he is the one who owns me."

Unwanted tears pricked my eyes and ran down my face, onto his hands. I hated crying. It was a waste of time and served no purpose. Cujo's thumbs swiped over my cheeks, wiping away the moisture and causing a shiver to run through me.

"Tell me where you live, Lily-Rose, and I will free you."

More tears came. "Then you would be the one who owns me. I still wouldn't be free."

Freedom. Something most people took for granted but wasn't something I'd ever expected to feel in my life.

Before he could respond, the outside door clanged open and Deputy Salvador came in, followed by another man I'd never seen before.

The deputy's anger was clear in his tone. "Dammit, Cujo, release her right this second. Lily-Rose, did he hurt you? Are you okay?"

With longing and regret in his eyes, Cujo dropped his hands away from my face, pulling out of my weak grip as he returned to his side of the bars.

"I will find you, Lily-Rose. You're mine."

His whispered words didn't carry far and I was sure the other two men, even with shifter senses, wouldn't have been able to hear him. I broke eye contact and turned to the deputy. "I'm fine. He didn't hurt me at all."

With that, I turned away from all three men and moved to the cot where I curled up and did my best to disappear into the wall. Cujo was a dream I couldn't afford to believe in. Even if he did save me from my father, what would it change? Instead of Kevin calling the shots, Cujo would. I still wouldn't be my own person. And even if Cujo found a way to free me from the bracelets, I wasn't sure I'd be able to shift. It'd been so long, and no one had taught me anything about my animal half. I'd only shifted once, that first time, and that had been an uncontrollable thing that had come out of nowhere and had ended with the bracelets being sealed over my wrists to prevent me from ever doing it again.

Chapter Three

Cujo

Reluctantly I turned away from Lily-Rose, surprised to see Joaquin was with Jaxson. "You made good time."

He shrugged. "Your lucky fucking day. I was in San Francisco on a run."

I nodded while Jaxson got busy unlocking then opening the cell door. "We'll head to an interview room."

Before leaving the cell block, I turned to get one last glimpse of my mate but winced at the sight she made curled up as small as she could get on that prison cot. She looked vulnerable and in need of protecting, a job I was discovering I wanted more and more.

The moment the door to the interview room was shut, Jaxson turned on me.

"If I find out you hurt that girl in any way, any deal we strike will be void and I will put you away. You understand me?"

I rolled my eyes before focusing in on the deputy. "I'd never fucking hurt Lily-Rose, but I do want to re-negotiate our deal. I want her to come with me."

Jaxson froze for a moment, like he was having trouble processing my words, before he shook free of the trance.

"You're something else, that's for sure. You're in no position to negotiate for a damn thing here. *I* have the upper hand, not you."

I pointed in the direction of the cell block. "That woman is mine. I won't fucking leave the area unless she's with me. Can't do it."

Joaquin cursed. "Only you'd manage to find your fucking mate in lock-up. Dammit, Cujo." He turned to Jaxson. "Sorry, but you know he's right. If she's his mate, he won't be able to leave. His wolf won't fucking let him. Who is she? Does she have anyone who'd try to stop her from leaving the area?"

Jaxson didn't take his glare off me, even as he responded to Joaquin. "Lily-Rose is a prostitute, although it's not by her choosing. We're all pretty sure she actively tries to get caught every so often so she can get a damn break. Her pimp — and father — will not let her go easily."

Joaquin folded his arms over his chest as he leaned back against the wall with a shake of his head, his disgust clear in his actions. I was feeling the same way about her father. What kind of parent sold his daughter like that?

Wondering how much Jaxson knew about her, I figured asking a few more questions wouldn't hurt.

"Do you know what her animal is?"

He shook his head. "With how she moves I'd guess feline, but no idea what type. Her bastard of a father locked down her shifter abilities early on. As far as the world is concerned, she's fully human."

I nodded. "She doesn't have any shifter in her scent. But she is definitely my mate. If she hadn't been near me during the night, you would have had to fucking tranq me at least two more times to keep me from escaping. She soothed my wolf and kept me calm. I fucking need her. And I can keep her safe from her father, give her a better life."

Jaxson pulled out a chair and sat down heavily. "I wish it was as simple as letting you take her out of the area with you, but it's not. Those bracelets of hers don't just dampen her abilities. I know they contain a tracker because her bastard of a father can always locate her and with how scared she gets whenever someone suggests she run away, I'm guessing they somehow keep her from straying too far away from him. So, me releasing her into your custody won't change a thing for her."

I shrugged. "I can take care of the bracelets. I trust the other information I gave you checked out?"

Jaxson was silent for a few minutes. Clearly, he had no fucking idea how to deal with me and my claims.

"Still digging but yeah, the information is going to give us some solid leads. How will you deal with the bracelets? The magic used is specifically targeted at shifters. No shifter can touch them without getting burned. I'm pretty sure only a magic user can remove them."

Copying Joaquin's position up against the wall, I gave the deputy a smug smile. After so many experiments to test my reaction to various types of magic, I was immune to most spells. "Magic isn't an issue for me. I'll get them off."

Jaxson shook his head again. "You're fucking crazy, aren't you?" He turned to Joaquin. "You sure you want to claim him?"

Joaquin nodded without hesitation. "The Iron Hammers MC is all about second chances for those of us who don't have anywhere else to go. He'll fit right in, as will his mate."

Jaxson huffed a breath. "Well, okay then." He pulled out some papers from a folder. "I'll need you to sign these, and there's a fine to pay. If you're taking care of Lily-Rose, she has an outstanding fine too."

Joaquin stepped away from the wall. "I'll go take care of the financial side of things while you get Cujo to sign everything."

Jaxson nodded. "Come back here when you're done. You need to sign too as his Alpha."

With Joaquin gone, Jaxson laid out the forms. "Can't believe I'm actually doing this. You're a fucking mercenary and I'm putting you back on the streets."

Strangely, my view on life had suddenly changed since finding Lily-Rose. She'd somehow unlocked the part of me that felt emotions and all that shit, so I found myself saying things to the deputy I never would have before meeting her.

"Taking Alina was simply a job. It wasn't anything personal. It's not like there's a whole lot of employment opportunities for a wolf like me. Man's gotta fucking eat. I've done what I had to do to survive, nothing more."

I took the pen offered and signed the forms, feeling Jaxson's stare on me the entire time.

"So you plan to keep doing what you do? Kidnapping, beat downs, assassinations... whatever the highest bidder wants to pay you for. Who says you're not going to turn that girl over to her father for a buck?"

Fury raced through my system and the pen snapped between my fingers, spilling ink over the table. I held Jaxson immobilized with my gaze.

"Don't you *ever* fucking imply that I'd ever hurt my mate or allow anyone else to harm her in any way. She will be cherished and protected for the rest of her days. As to what I intend to do for work, I guess that's up to Joaquin now, isn't it?"

Jaxson shifted the papers away from the inky mess, shaking his head. "Can't believe he's taking you on. I know full well he wasn't your Alpha before today."

"Yet you still called him."

He frowned at me. "Be grateful I want to get back to Alina more than I want to do all the paperwork required to keep you in here."

Joaquin returned and he raised an eyebrow at the black blot of ink on the table before taking another pen from Jaxson and signing the forms. Once that was finished, Jaxson stood. "You're free to go. Wait for me in the reception area. I'll bring Lily-Rose out to you in a few minutes."

I would have preferred to go with him to get her but realized he was bending the rules for me already and since I didn't want to risk him changing his mind, I went with Joaquin toward the front of the building.

"Thanks for coming for me."

Joaquin nodded. "Anytime, brother. You've always been welcome with the Iron Hammers, you know that. It's your lucky fucking day that a bunch of us were already in the area."

I shook my head. "Yeah, luck. You know where my SUV is? I should have asked the deputy about it."

Joaquin nodded. "Jaxson told me where it'd been towed. I had a couple of the men go pick it up for you. It should be out the front. Although, you're gonna need to get yourself a sled now that you're with us."

I shrugged off his suggestion. "I had a bike. Switched it out for an SUV for this last job."

Joaquin shook his head with a chuckle. "Yeah, well, your nomad days are fucking over. You can find a place in Galveston and settle down. With a home base you can own, however many vehicles you fucking want at the same time. No need to switch out your sled when you need a cage."

Her scent hit my nose and instantly had my full attention. Drawing a deep breath, I turned to watch as Jaxson led Lily-Rose toward us. She looked scared and her fear tainted her scent. Jaxson lowered his head and said something to her that didn't carry but she nodded and tentatively stepped toward me. I didn't wait for her to get to me, I strode over and wrapped an arm around her middle, pulling her in flush against my body, reveling in how peaceful I felt with her that close.

"C'mon, Lily-Rose, let's get the fuck outta here."

Shaking her head, she tried to pull away from my hold on her. "I can't go with you! It hurts if I'm too far away from him." She tugged at the bracelets. "No matter where I go, he'll be able to find me. The longer it takes him, the worse the beating will be. You have to leave me here."

Anger flashed hot through me. He beat her? I glared at Jaxson. "Some fucking deputy you are. Her father beats her. Pimps her out. And you do nothing? Law, my ass."

Jaxson's voice had more growl than normal. "This is the first I've heard about any beatings, and she's never been willing to press charges against her father. I have to follow the law. I need proof, witness statements... I can't just run off and haul people in, no matter how much I might want to."

With a shake of my head, I dismissed the deputy and his bullshit to focus on Lily-Rose. Releasing my hold on her waist, I lifted her right arm and after allowing a single wolf claw to grow from my index finger, sliced through the leather easily, tossing the now useless material into the trashcan in the corner. I quickly repeated the action on her left wrist, disposing of it in the same way.

I turned to Jaxson one last time. "You might want to burn those fuckers."

Then with a palm on her lower back, I guided my mate, who was staring at her wrists and touching the newly revealed skin like she couldn't quite believe I'd done what I said I would, outside. Joaquin followed us, chuckling.

When we got to the parking lot, there were six men all wearing Iron Hammer MC cuts waiting for us. Spotting my ride, I moved toward it and a man I recognized from when I'd done a job for Joaquin a while back stepped into my path. Chaos and I hadn't seen eye-to-eye on a couple of things. He was impulsive as hell and had a tendency to run headfirst into a situation with no escape plan.

"Keys are in it. There's not much in there, so not sure how much the cops stripped out on you. If you let me know what's missing, I can chase it up. See if we can't get it returned."

I shook my head. "There wasn't anything much in there to grab. Thanks."

He nodded toward Lily-Rose, who was still staring at her arms in awe. "Who's this? Entertainment for the road?"

Fury raced through my system and I pulled Lily-Rose so she was behind me. Joaquin stepped in front of me before I could knock the fucker's teeth in. "Back off her, Chaos. She's Cujo's mate, not a plaything."

That was the other thing Chaos was known for. The man had no fucking filter on his mouth.

· · • • • • • • · ·

Lily-Rose

He'd done it. He'd actually managed to remove the bracelets and accomplished it so easily. I was barely aware of the fact I was moving as I allowed Cujo to guide me outside the police station and into the parking lot. It wasn't until Cujo's fury hit me like a freight train a moment before he moved me behind him that I snapped out of my daze.

Clearly, the man standing in front of us had said something nasty that I'd not heard. The other man, the one who'd first come in to get Cujo with Deputy Jaxson, pushed in front of Cujo and shoved the other man further away, but I wasn't focusing on the drama. Not once I saw the back of the vest the man wore.

"Iron Hammers MC." My voice was barely a whisper as I repeated out loud those words I'd been taught to hate. It was the Iron Hammers MC who had taken my mother, drugged her up, raped her then sold her into human trafficking. Eventually she was bought by Kevin, who hadn't realized she was a shifter. Hadn't realized the birth control shot he insisted she get wouldn't work until she was pregnant with me.

My heart raced within my chest and my lungs burned as I struggled to breathe. I backed away from Cujo and everyone else. It wasn't difficult to do since everyone was focused on the impending fight between Cujo and the man who'd pissed him off. I stumbled when my foot hit the curb at the edge of the parking lot and at the sound, Cujo turned to face me. Within moments, I was the center of attention of all the men. All of whom, except for Cujo, wore a leather vest with Iron Hammers MC patches on it.

I shook my head, tears leaking from my eyes.

"No. Not with them."

The confusion that crossed Cujo's face caused an ache in my chest. He had no clue who these men were. But he'd been arrested last night. He'd done something illegal to have ended up in that cell, and I somehow doubted it was a crime like mine.

Emotion welled up and mixed with memories of my mother thrashing in her sleep with her nightmares from what their club had done to her. My cat hissed and rose up, bigger and stronger than she'd ever been before. Panic hit me for a moment before the shift took over, then I was on all fours within seconds.

"Lily-Rose!"

I turned to the sound of Cujo's voice and took a step toward him before the man beside him moved forward too. The sight of the Iron Hammers MC patch on his vest had my ocelot hissing again before she refused me any control and spun around then took off into the scrub and away from the men.

It was strange being in my animal form. I'd only ever experienced it one time before and I certainly hadn't had a chance then to go running or anything. I'd been playing in the big tree in our backyard, climbing way higher than I should have. When I slipped and fell, my ocelot rose up and I shifted before landing on all four feet, unharmed, on the ground. It seemed as though Kevin had been expecting me to shift at some point, because he'd had a bucket of foul-smelling liquid ready to go. He'd splashed it over me and as soon as it hit me, I shifted back to human against my will. I'd been coughing and spluttering from the liquid when he'd sealed the bracelets onto my wrists.

I ran until I was panting for breath, then finding a tall tree, I climbed as high as I could before I located a sturdy branch and curled in a ball and rested. The view from my perch was good and I was sure I'd see anyone coming at me before they saw me, giving me time to plan my next move.

For the first time in my life I was truly free. No bracelets meant that Kevin couldn't track me. I wasn't sure about Cujo's ability to locate me as my mate. Regardless, I needed to leave town. Kevin would search for me, and he'd be relentless. And even without the bracelets, if I stayed nearby, he'd eventually find me. I was near the coast, so that left me with north, east or south as options. The thought of going east toward Nevada had my ocelot growling, so that was out. For now, I'd go south. I might be able to make it down to the border and into Mexico. Surely, Kevin wouldn't go looking that far, and I could live out my life in this form in the jungle.

My cat purred with approval at that plan, so I rested my head on my paws and decided to risk having a short rest before I left on my journey.

Chapter Four

Cujo

Lily-Rose was spectacular in her animal form. Even after seeing her, I wasn't entirely sure exactly what she was. Her coat was spotted like a leopard, but smaller than any I'd ever seen. She was small enough I'd be able to hold her comfortably in my arms. If I ever saw her again.

I turned on Chaos and now that Joaquin wasn't standing between us, slammed my fist into his jaw. He dropped to the pavement like a rock, unconscious, which hadn't been my plan. I'd wanted to make him bleed some more before I knocked him out.

"For fuck's sake, Cujo. Really? Had to knock his ass out?"

I turned to Joaquin. "Would you prefer I kill the fucker?"

He rubbed a palm over his face, but I really didn't give a fuck if he was beginning to question his decision to take me in. I was out of jail so didn't care if he wiped his hands of me at this point. I shifted to my wolf and bounded over to where she'd disappeared into the shrubbery. Sniffing around, I found her scent. It was subtly different from how she'd smelled earlier, with a feline musk. Once I was locked onto her, I allowed my wolf to take over as I plowed into the ferns and redwoods and went after what was mine.

She would not escape me.

With my nose to the ground, I kept moving, following her trail and not caring about anything in my path. My low growl sent any wildlife scurrying as I went. She'd run a long way, and her little cat was damn fast. I quickly realized I wouldn't catch her until she stopped to rest. After a time, I became aware that three wolves were trailing me, I recognized Joaquin's scent, so I ignored them as I continued on the path to my mate.

When her scent vanished, I skidded to a stop, sniffing around to try to work out where she'd gone. A growl from above had me looking up into the tree canopy. She was tucked up high, way out of my reach. She appeared comfortable on her little perch and I doubted she planned on coming down any time soon.

Since we weren't mated yet, I couldn't communicate telepathically with her. I shifted to my human form so I could verbally attempt to convince her to come to me.

"Hey, sweetheart. You wanna come on down?"

The cat hissed at me before she set her head back on her paws. Her tail, which was shorter than I'd seen on other cats, swished angrily in the air. I sighed as I tried to think of something I could say that would convince her to leave her safe perch.

"I know what Chaos said had to make you think we were like your father, but we're not. He was just talking shit, running his mouth. You won't ever be forced to fuck anyone ever again." She raised her head and tilted it, as if asking a question that I completely understood. Dammit. "Yeah, that includes me. Although, I ain't gonna lie, I'll be doing everything I can to make it so you want to be with me."

She just blinked at me for a minute but she wasn't hissing or growling, so I was counting it as a win. Well, at least I was until Joaquin and the other two wolves with him arrived beside me and shifted. The moment they came into view, Lily-Rose's hackles went up and with her ears back, she began that low growl of hers again.

Joaquin held up his palms. "Whoa, little kitty. We mean you no harm. Your mate is right, we're not at all like your father. Chaos talks a lot of shit, but he'd never touch another man's woman. Hell, he'd never take any woman against her will."

When I noticed that Lily-Rose wasn't looking at Joaquin's face, I followed her gaze to see what held her attention. She was focused on Joaquin's chest, where his club patches were. I flipped my gaze up to his face as I started to put things together. "Joaquin, do you know what kind of cat she is?"

"An ocelot by the looks of it." He shifted his gaze from her to me. "Before you ask, yes, they were originally native to southern Texas."

"She's focused on your patches, not your face. I don't think this is about Chaos." I turned back to her. "Is that right, sweetheart? Is this about the Iron Hammers? Have you had dealings with them before?"

Her tail did another violent swish as she hissed at Joaquin and the two men standing beside him, all wearing club cuts. When I'd done work for Joaquin, he'd just taken over the club. There was mention of what the previous officers had done to earn their money.

Joaquin shook his head as he rested his hands on his hips. "This shit just keeps coming back to haunt us. Lily-Rose, my name is Joaquin Torres and along with some others, we took control of the Iron Hammers about four years ago. All those who had any part of the human trafficking the club did are dead and gone. It's a new group now, one that doesn't do that shit. In fact, we spend a lot of our time searching out those who were trafficked to save them. Ask your mate. He's helped us with it in the past. I promise you will come to no harm at the hands of the Iron Hammers MC. You'll only find protection."

She stopped hissing as he'd spoken, but that tail of hers was still swishing angrily. I wasn't sure what else to do to convince her to trust us enough to come down. She'd known me for less than a day. I couldn't expect her to believe me or Joaquin just because we said we were safe.

"Please, Lily-Rose. Come on down and give us a chance. We'll head back to Texas, far away from here and Kevin. We don't need to live with the club. We'll find a place out of town, somewhere on the coast where there's lots of trees and shit for you to climb around in. Your abilities aren't dampened any more. If we do anything you don't like, now you can fight back. You got claws, baby, and you're faster than any of us wolves."

Joaquin stepped forward again to speak to her. "We also have a few feline shifters in our club. While none of them are ocelots, I'm sure they'd be happy to spend time with you and help you figure out what your abilities and limits are. I'm guessing you've been forced to wear those bracelets for a long time and never had that chance."

He turned to me, frowning. "In that case, she might not know how to shift back to human. We'll leave you alone with her and head back to the motel. Once you get her down, even if she can't shift back yet, bring her there. We'll load up and make tracks back home."

· · · ● ● · ● ● · · ·

Lily-Rose

I stayed still as the three men shifted back to wolves and trotted away, keeping my gaze on them until they left my field of vision before I turned back to Cujo. Twitching my nose, I tried to inhale his scent but could only catch the barest hint of it from my position. He stayed motionless below my tree, just waiting. He didn't look angry, but he also didn't look like he was going to give up and leave any time soon.

Mate.

My ocelot stood firm. While she didn't have any trust or love for the Iron Hammers, Cujo was ours and apparently that was enough for her to trust him. Slowly I rose and digging my claws into the tree, made my way down the trunk to a lower branch. Once I was in a position to safely pause, I glanced up to check on his location. He hadn't moved but the moment he caught my gaze, he stepped forward, toward me. I was low enough in the tree that he could now reach me and with how he'd lifted his arms, I guessed that was his intention.

"That's it, sweetheart. You are a stunning kitty. So beautiful. We'll have you shift in front of a mirror someday so you can see for yourself. C'mon, come here and let me hold you for a bit. I promise you're safe with me."

He held his hands on either side of me, palms toward me, but didn't attempt to pick me up. I had my claws dug deep in the branch so he would have had a time trying to detach me anyway. I leaned over and sniffed at his palm, letting his scent soak into my lungs and soothe all the earlier panic I'd felt.

I nuzzled my head in against his hand, purring, and retracted my claws.

With a chuckle, he gathered me up and pulled me in against him. "There you go, safe and sound. How about we head to the motel and see about getting you to shift back? Since you shredded your clothes back in the parking lot, I'm thinking Joaquin had a point about you never being taught how to shift. It'll be easier for you to learn if you're in a safe environment with no distractions. And I'll ask Joaquin to find you something to wear. Neither me nor my wolf would handle others seeing you naked well at all."

He and Joaquin had guessed right. I'd never shifted voluntarily back to human before, and when

Kevin had forced the change on me, I hadn't done it with my clothes intact like these wolves could. Not that I cared about having shredded those slutty clothes Kevin forced on me. I would gladly never wear anything like that ever again.

Cujo started walking through the trees and with a contented purr, I rubbed myself against him. He chuckled when I bumped my head under his chin, nuzzling my face in against his neck, trying to absorb more of his scent. My feline instincts had taken over, and they were telling me I was safe in the arms of my mate, so I was free to relax and play a little.

"Affectionate little kitty, aren't you?"

He held me with one arm and used his other palm to stroke my back and sides as I continued to snuggle in against him. The caresses made me shiver in bliss as he strode quickly toward the town.

By the time we made it to the motel, I was purring like a train and pushing my head into his palm with each stroke he made down my body. But I stilled and grew silent when I caught sight of Joaquin and a few other men waiting for us.

"Shh, my little kitty. Everything's just fine. We need Joaquin to show us to a room, remember? And ask him for some clothes for you."

I stayed quiet and laid my ears down as I flicked my gaze between all the men, ready to pounce at any of them if they threatened Cujo or me.

"Lily-Rose, retract the claws."

Cujo's voice sounded a little strained and I looked down in shock to see I'd dug both front paws worth of claws into his shoulder. I quickly but carefully removed them from his flesh, before tearing part of his shirt away so I could lap at the wounds. My inner cat was in full control and my human side had no clue why she was doing what she was, but I was happy to see that apparently my saliva healed. Within moments, they were nothing more than rapidly fading pink dots.

When I glanced up again, Joaquin was watching us with a smirk on his face and a glint to his eyes, like he found this whole situation hilarious but didn't want to outwardly laugh.

"I see you two have made nice. Room nine is all yours. You'll find a change of clothes for you both in there already. We don't have much time to fucking waste here, so clean up as fast as you can. It's a couple days ride to get back to Galveston, and I want to make a good start on it today, if possible. No sense in making a fucking enemy out of the deputy if we don't have to. Never know when you'll need someone like that on your side."

I was totally on board with leaving as soon as possible. If Kevin hadn't figured it out yet, it wouldn't be long until he did. I'd like to be far away from Timber Cove when he started searching for me. I still wasn't one hundred percent sure I could trust the Iron Hammers MC, but my ocelot was refusing to even consider leaving our mate, so it looked like we were going to be hanging out with the Iron Hammers for now.

Joaquin handed Cujo a key card and after a muttered thanks, Cujo was taking me toward the room while I kept my gaze focused on the men who were all still watching us. I was grateful Joaquin hadn't stopped at the motel Kevin had made me work out of, a run-down-should-have-been-condemned-twenty-years-ago place on the other side of town. Kevin never spent any money he didn't absolutely have to when it came to anything other than his own comfort.

Once we were inside the surprisingly spacious room, Cujo kicked the door shut and headed toward the bed. When he loosened his grip, I reluctantly leaped to the mattress where I stretched out before with a swish of my tail, I turned around to sit and watch my mate. He was very tall, with wide shoulders. His dark hair was cropped short and he had a closely trimmed beard that drew my attention to his mouth, which began to stir other ideas.

"Right, well. As fucking adorable as you are in this form, I need you to shift back so we can get cleaned up and head out." He rubbed a palm over the back of his neck. "Assuming Joaquin hit it on the head, and you haven't done this in a long time." He winced. "I haven't had to think about *how* I shift in a long damn time. You sort of just picture yourself as a human, with arms and legs, fingers and toes, all that shit. And it happens."

I frowned. What about clothes? But I couldn't ask until after I shifted. The downside to being an animal was the lack of voice. Looking around, I saw a pile of clothes on the desk. I pointed my nose toward it then looked back to Cujo, trying to get him to guess what I wanted. He followed my gaze after the second time and grinned.

"You shredded your clothes when you shifted, so you're gonna be naked when you shift this time. I'm not sure how ocelot magic works with stuff like clothes, but for me, it took some practice. It didn't take long to harness the magic needed to shift my clothes with me."

I did not want him to see me naked for the first time here in a motel room with a bunch of bikers outside waiting on us. Quickly, I turned and tucking my paw under the neatly made bed, I shoved the bedding down, intending on nosing under the sheet before I tried to shift.

Chapter Five

Cujo

I couldn't hold back my laughter. Watching Lily-Rose in her cat form try to crawl under the bed covers was one of the cutest damn things I'd ever seen. She stilled when I started to chuckle, then turned to glare and hiss at me.

"Oh, c'mon, sweetheart. You gotta know how funny you look trying to get into bed as a cat. You don't want me to see you naked?"

She lowered her head and if a cat could blush, she would, I was sure. As much as I'd fucking love to drag this out and keep playing with my mate, we had places to be. Moving to the bed, I pulled the blankets off until I had the sheet free and clear.

"I'll hold this up between us and you can grab it to wrap around yourself after you shift, okay?"

Hopefully, she'd think I was going to keep the sheet up so I'd only be able to see her face. The way she sat there, blinking up at me like she was waiting for something else, indicated I was shit-out-of-luck on that happening.

"I ain't turning around, Lily-Rose. This is as good as you're gonna fucking get. Deal with it."

She was my fucking mate and I wanted to see every inch of her. I wanted to lick, nip and touch every inch of her too, but that would have to wait. I also wanted to watch her shift. When she'd changed earlier, it had been a sudden, emotion-charged transformation that I'd barely caught sight of. Every animal shifted in a slightly different manner, and I was damn curious how she'd differ from me.

With a little huff, she closed her eyes and lowered her head, hopefully focusing on changing. A rain of amber sparks began to swirl around her a moment before her body began to transform, growing and lengthening until she was kneeling on the bed in her human form.

Instantly, my mouth watered at the sight of her sitting there, lush tits out, nipples tight in the coolness of the room's air conditioning. As much as I didn't want to cover her sexy-as-fuck body, I moved forward and wrapped the sheet around her. The moment I made contact, her eyes flew open on a gasp, as though she hadn't realized she'd managed to shift until that moment. And fuck me, but when the tip of her tongue ran over her bottom lip, I wanted to follow it with my own and find out if she tasted as good as she smelled.

"Let's get you in the shower. You'll feel better once you're clean."

Although her shift had removed any dirt she had on her, a shower would help relax her muscles. Hurt flashed across her eyes as she snatched the sheet out of my hands and finished tucking it around her after she slipped off the bed. Instinct had me reaching out to soothe her. Wrapping my arm around her waist, I gathered her in against me. Sliding a palm up her spine, I tangled my fingers in her long, blonde locks and pulled her head back until she was looking me directly in the eyes. She couldn't fail to notice how hard my cock was. My jeans did fuck all to hide the damn thing.

"Don't doubt for a fucking second how much I want you. And I *will* show you. But not here, and not now. When I come inside you for the first time, it'll be when I have all fucking night to make sure you know you want to belong to me, we clear?"

With her mouth open, she silently blinked up at me like I'd shocked her, but at least she wasn't looking hurt or rejected anymore. Unable to resist getting at least a small taste of my mate, I lowered my head. Lapping my tongue over her plush bottom lip, I sucked it into my mouth and gave it a light tug before releasing it and taking her mouth in a kiss I knew would leave her lips swollen and marked with my possession. A shiver ran up my spine as her small hands crept around my waist, slipping under my shirt to sear my skin with her scorching touch.

Giving up on my idiotic idea to put off claiming her, I pulled from her lips long enough to tear the sheet off her body and the shirt from mine, then I was back on her, my lips against hers as I lifted her. She wrapped her arms around my neck and her legs around my waist, her slick pussy pressing against my abs having me nearly losing my fucking mind. She was wet and warm, ready to be fucked. And my cock was hard enough to pound nails... more than ready to claim this little bombshell for my own.

With a growl, I spun us and had her up against a wall while I reached around her legs to get to the fly on my pants so I could free my cock that was aching with my need for her. Ending the kiss, I nipped at her chin before moving up her jawline, nibbling her soft skin as I went.

"I thought—" She shuddered when I got to her ear and tugged on the delicate little lobe. "Thought you said you wouldn't fuck me till we had all night."

Before I responded, I ran my nose down the side of her neck, then licked at the spot I wanted to mark before I responded.

"I underestimated how strong the mating fever would be. I don't think I'm gonna be able to fucking think straight till I have my cock in you." Pulling away from her throat, I ran my gaze down her body, taking in the flush that had spread from her face, down across her chest. Her tits were moving with her every breath and her beaded nipples had my mouth watering for a taste. Without another thought, I wrapped my hands around either side of her waist and hauled her up the wall higher. She squealed at the sudden movement and gripped my shoulders tighter when I took the first of her nipples deep into my mouth and sucked hard on it.

"Oh, mmm..." She hummed and ground her pussy against my abs.

I swirled my tongue around the tight bud then released it from my mouth so I could blow air over the wet flesh. When I switched to her other breast and did the same thing to that one, she whimpered and shifted her grip to my hair. I wasn't sure if she was pulling me closer or pushing me away. Her skin tasted like the honeysuckle that dominated her unique scent and the longer I licked and suckled on her tits, the more I wondered what her cream would taste like.

Aware we had limited time, I reluctantly lifted my mouth away from her skin and looked up into her face.

"Wish I had all fucking day to spend just sucking on your tits, babe. But we don't, so this is gonna be hard and fast."

She smiled at me and moved her hand to cup my jaw, rubbing her soft skin against my short beard. "It's all I've ever had, Cujo. You don't need to worry about me."

A growl ripped from my throat as a red-hot fury slammed through me. Not only had her piece of shit father pimped her out, no one had ever taken his time with her. I bet that shit went further than just sexually speaking, too. That was something we had in common. I'd been stolen as a cub and put through over a decade of experiments and tests. There'd been no Alpha to guide me, no mother for comfort. Lily-Rose and I weren't so different from each other.

"That changes here and now. You will *never* be left wanting. Not in any way. I will always fucking take care of you. Not just sexually, but in every way you need."

Tears welled in her eyes and she sucked in her lower lip and bit down on it.

"You don't believe me?"

She winced, "Why would you want to? Not even my own parents—"

"Don't want to ever hear you fucking mention them again. They never deserved to have a child, especially not one as sweet as you. You're mine now, and I've got you fucking covered."

She leaned in and kissed the corner of my mouth. "One day you're going to tell me what happened in your past that's made you so understanding, but I don't think Joaquin is going to give us that long today."

I shook my head as I turned and moved to the bed where I lowered her down gently until she was laying sprawled out like a sexy pin-up waiting for me.

"He'll give us long enough for me to fucking claim you because I don't think my wolf will cope with having you around all those men if I haven't left my fucking mark on you."

With a wide grin, she held her hands out to me.

"You better get down here and get marking then, babe. Before we run out of time."

Damn, but I was one lucky motherfucker. No matter how willing she was to have this first go-round hard and fast, I wasn't going to give in. Joaquin was just going to have to fucking wait a little longer to get out of Timber Cove because I intended to get a nice long taste of my mate and make her scream a time or two before I claimed what was mine.

· · · • • • • • · ·

Lily-Rose

Holy shit. Was this man—er, shifter—even real? I was tempted to pinch myself to check I was awake. Maybe I'd fallen asleep in lock-up and was dreaming. Before I could act on it, he'd shoved my legs open wider and lowered down between them.

"What are you do—" I didn't even get to finish my question before he took a long lick up through my pussy lips and stole not only my breath but my sanity too. Nothing in my entire life had ever felt that good.

I relaxed against the soft mattress as he continued to make a meal out of me. When he started thrusting his fingers in and out of me while he alternated between suckling and gently biting at my clit, I bowed off the bed, right on the verge of coming. My legs shook as the spiral of arousal built within me. Opening my mouth to pant, I saw stars sparkle through my vision for a few moments before all I saw was white while my body blew apart with an intense orgasm like I'd been shattered into a million pieces and was floating around the room.

Cujo's soft lips gently caressing mine brought me back to reality. With a sigh, I returned his kiss, loving how he tasted, how he felt over me, surrounding me with his strength. For the first time in my life, I didn't feel trapped when a man crawled over me. My body was humming with bliss from the orgasm, leaving me feeling drunk. I could stay here like this forever.

I whimpered when he ended the slow, drugging kiss, and through hooded eyes watched as he moved to kneel between my spread legs. With a grin and a gleam in his eye, he ran his large palms down my shoulders, over my breasts, tweaking my nipples quickly before he moved on to wrap a palm around either side of my waist. He paused and looked up into my face, waiting until I met his gaze.

"Tell me you want this. That you accept me."

I really wanted to know his history. Someone had done a number on his self-worth at some point as well as his body. His skin was covered in scars that he'd done his best to hide with ink. My ocelot rose her head up with a growl. She wanted to go hunting, to seek vengeance for our mate.

He tightened his grip, jolting me from my thoughts. His voice was a low, sexy growl. "Fucking answer me, mate."

Lifting up until I could cup his face between my palms, I ran my nose down the side of his before lightly kissing his lips. "I want this. I want to spend my life with you. I promise, your heart is safe with me. I won't ever hurt you."

His hands slipped around to my back until he could pull me in tightly against his chest. His muscles bunched tight as he squeezed me almost to the point I couldn't catch a full breath. I wrapped my arms around his neck, running my fingers through his thick hair, loving how it felt against my skin.

Rubbing my cheek against his, I enjoyed the softness of his beard for a moment before I whispered near his ear. "Claim me, mate. I'm yours for the taking."

He quickly adjusted our position so his cock head was resting at my entrance.

"Look at me."

Unable to resist his order, I locked my gaze with his as he pulled me down over his thick erection. He was big everywhere, including his cock, but I was so wet from his earlier attentions, he slid in easily, as though I truly had been made for him. After enjoying the feel of him filling me for a few moments, I squeezed my inner muscles as I swiveled my hips over him.

"Fuck." Before the word was out of his mouth, he had me flat on my back and was pounding into me, his fingers digging into my hips. Every stroke lit me up, pushing me closer to coming again. I reached out to grip his shoulders to keep myself grounded under the onslaught of his possession. Before I knew it, my body was tipping over the edge again, shattering beneath him.

His low growl had me turning my neck to him, whimpering in anticipation. He struck quickly, sinking his wolf teeth into the junction of my neck and shoulder. The moment he pierced my skin, his cock jerked within me as he started to fill me with his cum, causing me to climax again. Crying out at the power that was swirling through me, I had to force my brain to focus enough for me to lean up and sink my own teeth into him. His blood hit my tongue like whiskey, burning the whole way down to my gut.

When I was able, I withdrew and lapped at the wound, sealing it closed as he did the same to me. I flopped down on the mattress, unable to move, grinning up at Cujo. My mate. Dropping down on his elbows, he brushed my hair away from my face and kissed me gently, so different from the sex we'd just had.

"Mine."

I hummed at his claim, pleasure flowing through me at the knowledge this big, strong, sexy-as-hell, wolf shifter had claimed me for his. I knew allowing him to claim and mark me wasn't going to instantly fix everything, and that we'd still need to deal with my father at some point, but for now, everything was right in my world.

Chapter Six

Cujo

It'd been a struggle to leave Lily-Rose alone in the bathroom to shower and dress, but I knew if I didn't go, I'd end up fucking her again and we needed to get out of this shit-hole before her father came looking. Not that I was scared of the human asshole. I simply didn't want to get on the deputy's radar again by killing a human in his territory. Ideally, I'd like to make it back to the Iron Hammers MC clubhouse where I could lock her down, knowing she was safe. Then I'd go fucking hunting. The man who'd caused so much pain to my mate was going to die slowly and painfully. It was the least he deserved for all he'd done.

Closing the door gently behind me, I turned to see someone had driven my SUV over here, which I was grateful for. At least until I noticed who the fuck was leaning against it.

"Finally. Where's the girl? You fuck her to death?"

I flipped off Chaos, who thanks to his shifter genetics had fully recovered from me knocking him out earlier.

"Fuck off. Where's Joaquin?"

Chaos stayed where he was, grinning like the fucking moron he was. "He had to take a call. He'll be back any second now."

Not wanting to be social with the fucker I already wanted to knock out again, I turned back to the room, intending on waiting for Lily-Rose to be ready to go before coming outside again.

"Yo, Cujo! Hold up."

At Joaquin's voice, I stopped with a hand on the door handle and turned to watch as the president of the Iron Hammers and my new Alpha strode toward me. "Lily-Rose is just showering. She'll be right to go soon."

Joaquin nodded. "You claimed her?"

Taking a step away from the room, I braced myself for a fight. I didn't give a flying fuck if he was now my Alpha. No way would I apologize for anything that had happened earlier between me and my mate.

"Calm the fuck down. Damn, you always this quick to jump to conclusions? I don't have an issue with you claiming your mate. To be honest, I'd prefer it. Means I don't have to put up with you in a mating-heat haze getting jealous over every little fucking thing the rest of us do the whole way home."

I folded my arms across my chest, but didn't stop paying attention to what every man in the parking lot was doing. "Figured you'd be at least a little pissed off that we didn't rush back out here."

Joaquin shrugged with a smirk. "Brother, I got a woman back home waiting for me. Trust me, I get what it's like when you meet your mate. I told you to hurry the fuck up so you wouldn't drag it out. Last thing any of us want is you two chasing each other's tails the whole trip back." He held up his finger, "That said, we do really need to get moving. Don't want the good deputy to catch on we're not doing like we told him we would."

Right at that moment, a cop car drove past out on the road. Slow enough it was obvious he was checking up on us.

"For fuck's sake, he couldn't have expected us to just up and go straight away, not once Lily-Rose was with us."

He nodded out toward the road. "That's the third car I've seen so far. None have been Jaxson, but it won't take long before they pull him in to come deal with us if we don't get moving."

The door swinging open beside us had me turning to face that direction, inhaling deeply of my mate's fresh scent, which now had a hint of my own mixed in with it. Grinning like a damn fool at that fact, I reached for her and tugged her out of the doorway and in against me.

"You smell so fucking good."

I nuzzled in against her hair until a gagging noise had me turning to Chaos, letting my fangs drop as I growled.

"Put it away, Cujo. For fuck's sake, enough with the PDAs. Let's get rolling."

He turned and headed over to the row of bikes, the other men following him except Joaquin who was, once again, chuckling.

Choosing to ignore Chaos and his drama, I got down to business.

"What route are you planning on taking?"

Now it was his turn to cross his arms over his chest. "Figured we'd go as direct as we can. Through Arizona, New Mexico then into Texas. You got any issues with that plan?"

I shook my head, "No problem at all."

Joaquin grunted before he turned and rose his voice so everyone could hear. "Load up and let's get this fucking show on the road!"

Once we were a good way out of town, Lily-Rose turned away from the window and faced me. "How long has Joaquin been your Alpha?"

I glanced in her direction briefly before focusing back on the road and the bikes in front of us. "Today is the first day."

Silence filled the cab when I didn't say anything more. She didn't let it stay that way for long though.

"And you suddenly decided to join his pack because?"

I shrugged a shoulder. "Jaxson would only go through with a deal if I left with an Alpha who took responsibility for me. Joaquin was the only one I could think of who might have taken me in. And thank fuck he did."

An involuntary shudder ran through me at the thought of having to spend years in jail.

· · • • • • • · · ·

Lily-Rose

This man did not like to talk. All I wanted was to get to know him, his history, how he ended up where he was now. But it was like pulling teeth. All these short answers. But I was determined to get to know my mate, so bring on question time. We had a two-day drive ahead of us with nothing other than the occasional stop to interrupt me.

"What deal was that exactly? What did you do to get arrested?"

His grip on the steering wheel tightened a moment before he blew out a breath.

"I'm a mercenary of sorts. I'll do whatever the client wants. In this case, the client wanted me to bring a woman to a particular place."

I rolled my eyes at him trying to make what he did sound better than it obviously was. "You kidnapped a woman. Just say it. You didn't hurt her, did you?"

I didn't want to believe I mated a man who would hurt a woman, but what did I really know about this male?

"She's totally healthy and intact. Jaxson wanted to know who I was working for more than he wanted to lock me up, so I bartered with him to get my charge lowered down to a fine rather than going to jail. You saw how my wolf handles cages. It doesn't end well."

I started to chew on my right index fingernail as I thought about how to ask him what I wanted to know. Would he tell me? He seemed like a fairly private person, but I was his mate. Surely, he wouldn't try to hide his past from me? I decided to leave it for now.

"How did you know Joaquin would accept you?"

He shrugged again. "I didn't, but he's the only Alpha I know that there was a fucking chance he'd step up."

"So, when did you meet Joaquin?"

He frowned over at me before turning his attention back to the road. "You ask a lot of fucking questions, you know that?"

I grinned. "You give short answers, so I have to."

He shook his head, but I could see his lips twitch with a grin he was trying to hold back.

"I did a job for him a while back. He was searching for a female who'd been trafficked. I helped out with some investigative work. He actually offered me a place in his pack back then, but I turned it down."

He went silent again and when I sighed, his lips did that twitch thing again. Was he playing with me? I mentally shrugged, like it mattered. He was answering my questions, even if he was forcing my hand in asking him more than I should have to, and that's what was important here. He was also proving he had a sense of humor, which I didn't mind one bit. My feline half loved playing.

"So Mr. Lone Wolf, does that mean you don't intend on staying with the Iron Hammers?"

His entire body stiffened and with a low growl he shook his head.

"Originally that was my plan, to leave as soon as we were away from Timber Cove, but that's all changed now. I'd never risk you like that."

I frowned. "Risk me?" I'd have thought staying with the Iron Hammers was the risky thing to do. I only had Joaquin's word to go on that they'd changed from what they used to be.

Cujo nodded. "My parents were both shifters, living up in Boseman, Montana. But they had no pack. I was two years old when the hunters found us. Mom shielded me as best she could while Dad fought them off, but there were too many of them. He never stood a chance. None of us did."

My heart lurched in my chest. Clearly, he'd survived, but how? "What happened? Are your parents still alive?"

He shook his head and I wanted to reach out and hug him, do something to ease the pain that was clear to read in the tense line of his muscles. "The hunters killed them both, but kept me alive. They sold me to a bunch of scientists."

How were you meant to respond to information like that? I said the first thing that came to mind. "Hope you killed the fuckers."

He barked out a laugh and I relaxed that I'd said the right thing.

"Yeah, sweetheart. Took me twenty-six years but I did kill all those fuckers on my way out."

That had me stilling, dumbfounded at what he'd said. "They had you for twenty-six years?"

"Yeah, whatever you're imagining, it was worse. I wasn't the only shifter they got their hands on, but I was the only one that got out alive. And that's why my wolf reacts like he does to cages of any sort."

I nodded, still shocked. "Makes sense. So how old are you now?"

He raised an eyebrow as he glanced at me. "Worried I'm too old for you now, babe? Age differences don't mean a fucking thing between mates."

I rolled my eyes, the tension of his earlier revelation broken with his joking. "I'm well aware we're bonded now. I just wanted to know how old you were out of curiosity."

"I'm thirty-six. So, been free of that hell hole for eight years now. How about you, my curious little kitty, how old are you?"

I had no clue how he was going to react to my age. He might have joked that I was going to have an issue with the age gap, but I honestly didn't care. However, he might when he found out how young I was.

"Well, remember my age in years is far different to how old I am, if you get my meaning."

He gave me another of his side-eye glances. "Just fucking tell me already."

"I'm nineteen."

The car swerved as Cujo jolted. "Motherfucking-son-of-a-bitch!"

I gripped the handle above the door and winced as his inventive cursing continued while he regained control of the SUV. Yep, as I'd guessed... he was not happy about my age. Was it possible to break a mate bond once it was sealed? I wasn't sure. Tears filled my eyes as the bikes ahead of us pulled into a truck stop off the highway and Cujo followed, pulling up behind them.

Chapter Seven

Cujo

Skidding the car to a stop behind the bikes, I rocketed out the door, slamming it. Still cursing a blue streak, I started to pace the parking lot to the side of the truck stop. No one came near me, which was fucking great. Mood I was in, I'd kill someone.

I wanted to kill her piece of shit father. Nineteen years old. A fucking baby and she'd been a hooker for how long? Hell wasn't hot enough for that asshole. I stormed back over to the car, ripping her door open. She cringed away from me and it was like a blade through my heart. I'd never fucking lay a hand on her, but I couldn't get the words out to reassure her. My wolf wanted out, he wanted to go hunt.

"How long has he been pimping you out?"

She blinked up at me and the tears running down her cheeks were another blade through me, but I couldn't comfort her yet. I had energy and rage that needed to be burned off first, and I needed to know this information. If I didn't find out now, I'd just flip my lid again later when she told me. Better to get it all out now.

"Fourteen years."

She whispered the words so quietly, if I hadn't been a shifter, I wouldn't have heard her. But I did. And as I did the math, rage like I'd never felt poured like lava through me.

"Five? That motherfucking piece of shit started selling you out at five fucking years old?"

Turning away, I stormed over to the edge of the lot facing out over the landscape. I wanted to howl. My wolf wanted out, wanted to go hunting right fucking now and tear that piece of shit apart. Gravel crunching had me swinging my attention to the side to where Joaquin was approaching me with measured steps. I knew he could move silently so the fact I'd heard him meant he wanted to alert me of his presence. As he got closer, I turned my body to face him fully. "She's still a fucking baby, Joaquin. Nineteen years old and that motherfucking asshole has been pimping her out for fourteen fucking years. Who the fuck sends out his five-year-old daughter to fuck men?"

He shook his head, his expression grim. "A monster, that's who. We'll make him pay. We will find a way to take him down. But not here, not now.

Your mate needs your comfort right now. Not your rage."

His eyes flashed to his Alpha blue as he reached out and gripped my shoulder. Instantly my wolf was soothed, which freaked me out enough I pulled away.

"What the fuck did you just do?"

Confusion clouded his eyes a moment before they cleared. "You don't know?"

I shook my head. "Know what? I've never had an Alpha. You looked into my past. You know I wasn't raised in a pack."

He cleared his throat. "As your Alpha, I can help you by drawing away things like strong emotions or pain. I was taking some of your rage so you could calm the fuck down before you did something stupid. It's not safe to shift here. We'll grab some lunch, then get back on the road. We got another few hours of riding before we'll reach the motel I'm aiming for. Once we get settled, you'll be able to go for a run. We all can. But right now, that ain't happening. Get your wolf under control." He pointed over to my car, where the other Iron Hammers were surrounding it, keeping my woman protected. "She had to live with that fucker. She's had fourteen years of abuse and torture at his hands. You, of all people, know what that's like. You've had years to adjust to being free, but today is her first taste of being rid of him. Don't cut her down before she has a chance to learn to fly, brother. Take a deep breath, shove that rage down for now and go be the mate she needs you to be."

I hadn't lied to Joaquin. My parents had been rogue wolves, not part of a pack. So even before I was taken as a cub, I hadn't ever had a pack and Alpha. Of course, I'd heard stories over the years, but this was the first time I'd experienced it firsthand. It was rather disconcerting to not be the one in control of my feelings. In the past, if I got mad, I shifted and ran it off. Or found someone who needed hunting down to vent my rage on. Maybe being part of a pack and having an Alpha would do more than just provide extra protection for my mate and any offspring we might have. Maybe I didn't need to live with my wolf's baser instincts dictating how I responded to things.

Now that Joaquin had siphoned off some of my rage, I was calmer and could think. "We should turn around. Go back and fucking hunt him down. End him."

He folded his arms over his chest as he shook his head. "Not a good idea. Jaxson won't hesitate to come after you. He'll have you locked up in a heartbeat if something happens to Kevin. And we don't fucking need to chase him. Sounds to me like your mate was how he pulled an income. He's not going to be happy about losing her for that reason alone. But even without that, trust me, he'll follow us. When he does, we can take that fucker out on our home turf where no one will ever know what happened to him."

That had me frowning. "How can you be so fucking sure he'll come after us? We're traveling over three state lines, for fuck's sake."

Folding his arms over his chest, he smirked at me. "I'll tell you all about Daniela another time. For now, go to your mate. Once she's calm, we'll head inside and grab some lunch."

With that, he turned and walked over toward the diner attached to the truck stop, half of the men following while the other half stayed where they'd been. After taking a deep breath, I headed toward my SUV. Opening her door, I winced at the sight of her. She'd pulled her knees up and wrapped her arms around them. Her eyes were red, and tears still tracked down her face. Fuck, what could I say or do to fix this? I shouldn't have stormed off, but I didn't know what else to do to protect her from my rage.

· · · • • · • • · ·

Lily-Rose

Cujo wincing at me had me wondering about whether I could shift and slip out the door around him. Run away into the trees that surrounded this parking lot. Those thoughts fled when Cujo moved closer, and fear rose up to consume me as I flinched away from him.

"Just let me go and I'll leave. You never have to see me again."

He jerked as though I'd punched him. "What the fuck do you mean? Let you go? You agreed to be mine. We're bonded fucking mates. You don't get to give up on this!"

Swallowing hard, I unclipped my seat belt and tried to move further away from his fury.

"Please don't hurt me."

I was mortified to be reduced to begging. It had never made a damn difference before, but I couldn't stop trying. I hated how Kevin would beat me till I could barely walk, relying on my shifter healing – which the bracelets didn't limit – to make it so I'd be able to work the following night. Unfortunately, being able to heal quickly didn't make the blows hurt any less.

"Fuck me. Sweetheart, I won't ever raise a hand to you in anger. Not ever. Nor will I ever give up on us. I didn't walk away from you just now, Lily-Rose, I walked away to vent my rage away from you. I'm fucking furious at your father, not you. Never you."

After wiping my tears on my shirt sleeve, I looked up into his eyes, trying to gauge if he was being honest. "For real? You don't want to break off the mating?"

A flash of pain passed through his gaze. "Sweetheart, that's not how mating bonds work. There's no such thing as divorce in our world. We're bonded. Forever. But even if that wasn't how it worked, I wouldn't pass you over for anything. Least of all because you've been the victim of abuse all your life. Fuck that." He reached his hand toward me, holding it out, waiting for me to either accept or reject him. After taking a deep breath for courage, I placed my palm against his and he closed his fingers around mine, tugging until I uncurled from the seat and moved to exit the vehicle. As soon as I was standing, he switched his grip to my hips and lifted me up. Out of reflex, I wrapped my legs around his waist and my arms around his neck the moment my feet left the ground.

"What are you doing?"

My voice came out breathless as I stared into his eyes, the silver threaded through the ice blue holding me mesmerized as he smirked.

"I'm fixing what I fucked up. Gonna kiss you senseless, then we'll go eat."

Sliding his hand up my back until his fingers were tangled in my hair, he tugged gently until my face was where he wanted it. When his lips pressed against mine, everything in me relaxed, loosened, as a wave of contentment flowed through me.

Followed rapidly by a blast of arousal that I knew we couldn't do a damn thing about. Yet.

Chaos' voice was laced with humor. "Cujo, get off that poor woman before I find a bucket of water to toss over you to save her."

As Cujo pulled away with a growl, I couldn't help but burst out laughing. These men were ridiculous, and it was just what I needed to reset my thoughts. When Cujo lowered my feet to the ground, still growling at Chaos, I took his face between my palms until he looked back at me.

"Let it go, Cujo."

He stared into my eyes for a few moments before the tension drained from his body and he stepped back, taking my hand in his as he began to walk toward to the diner connected to the truck stop.

Once we were all inside and seated, a waitress came and took our orders. After she disappeared, chatter rose up between all the men. Clearly, they were all anxious to head home. It made me curious about what they'd been doing on their run, but I didn't want to risk pissing off anyone by asking.

Joaquin was sitting on the other side of Cujo and as though my mate had heard my thoughts, he turned to Joaquin.

"What the fuck were you doing that had you conveniently close by when I needed you?"

Joaquin raised an eyebrow and smirked. "Because Daniela told us that's where we needed to be."

Another of the men, who had a patch that read Illusion, nodded. "That female ain't ever wrong. We've learned to listen."

I frowned. "Who is Daniela? I thought MCs were all men."

All the men chuckled but it was Joaquin that answered. "Daniela isn't technically a member of the club. And while only men are brothers within the Iron Hammers MC, none of us pretend for a moment that our women aren't just as fucking important as we are."

The waitress returned with a coffee pot and filled cups before heading off again. Joaquin waited for her to be out of earshot before he continued,

"Daniela is a very special female. One we're extremely lucky to have on our side."

Cujo took a mouthful of his coffee before he cleared his throat. "She a witch?"

Joaquin shrugged. "Of a sort. We found her on a raid and rescued her."

Illusion laughed. "Nearly left her behind thinkin' she was part of the wildlife."

Another round of chuckles had me frowning again. Clearly, Cujo was getting as frustrated as I was.

"Just fucking tell me who or what she is. I don't fucking do games."

Joaquin sighed. "Relax, Cujo. You have no patience. Daniela is a Brazilian Rainbow Boa shifter. She comes from a long line of powerful magic users."

I shook my head. "If she's a powerful magic user, why did she need rescuing?"

I'd wished so many times I'd been born a witch. That would have meant being able to break free of the bracelets.

Joaquin turned his focus to me. "No magic is limitless, Lily-Rose. Daniela was caught in her animal form and brought to the States to be sold as an exotic pet. While she's bigger than a normal Rainbow Boa, her animal form is still a lot smaller than her human half. Her captors kept her in a cage too small for her to shift. In her snake form, her magic is limited. She was unable to escape on her own."

I was still confused. "So, the ones that took her didn't know she was a shifter? Why take a snake if they didn't know what she was?"

Illusion spoke up again, "The Rainbow Boa is a stunning animal. Its scales are iridescent. The species was nearly wiped due to being captured and sold as pets. We assume that's how Daniela was caught, but she don't talk about it much so we don't know for sure. If you want to know more about her, you'll have to ask her yourself. Although, like I said, she don't talk much so I doubt you'll get many answers."

Joaquin took back over. "I'm sure you'll meet her soon after we roll into town. She was very worked up over us needing to come to San Fran to wait for a call. As Illusion said, she's never fucking been wrong yet. She's a big help with our raids."

These men were as bad as Cujo. Half answers that gave me more questions. "Raids?"

He grinned. "Several of us who took over the Iron Hammers MC descend from Vikings. We like to honor our ancestors and keep doing what they started. We go raiding to save those caught up in human or shifter trafficking. Since Daniela's been helping us, we've been more successful, but we weren't doing half bad before either."

The waitress came out and started delivering all the food, so I sat back and processed everything I'd learned. I couldn't wait to meet Daniela. She sounded like an extremely interesting woman. Learning about the raiding the club now did, I was beginning to believe Joaquin that the club had changed from who they used to be when my mother was taken and held by them.

Chapter Eight

Lily-Rose

It was early evening the following day when we finally rolled into Galveston. I'd been a toddler when Kevin fled this place and I had no memories of anything here. That didn't stop me from being nervous the closer we got to the Iron Hammers clubhouse. For all of Joaquin's verbal reassurances, I still wasn't one hundred percent sure he was speaking the truth. I wanted to believe he was. Wanted to believe this was the start of a new, happier life for me.

Cujo reached over and rested his palm on my thigh, his heat soaking in and soothing me a little. "You doing okay, sweetheart?"

I pulled my fingers away from my mouth. I really needed to stop chewing my nails. Not only did it make my hands look like crap, but it was like a neon sign to the world that my mind was a mess.

"Just nervous about what we're going to find at the clubhouse."

He nodded. "Can understand that. After Kevin took your mom from the club, did they stay here? Is this where you were born?"

I turned to face him. He really was a gorgeous man. His short beard did nothing to hide the strong line of his jaw or his completely kissable lips. When he flicked a quick glance my way, my cheeks heated at being busted ogling him.

"Yes, I was born here. I was a toddler when we moved, so I don't have any memories of Galveston. I have a few from our time in New Mexico." A shudder ran through me.

He glanced my way again, frowning. "What happened?"

Would telling him have him losing his temper again? I sighed. He'd want to know eventually, so I might as well just get it all out now.

"From what I've heard the other women say over the years, I think I've pieced together most of what happened in those early years. Kevin drove a taxi here in town. Somehow, that led to him getting in with an Iron Hammer. The club gave Kevin my mom in payment for him bringing others to them, which he was obviously more than happy about. Then, in 2002, a group formed that was saving girls from the club. Kevin managed to join up with this group and he then would grab some of the girls they saved to sell himself."

He growled. "Bet the club was happy about that. Fucker."

"Well, the entire crew ended up dead aside from him, so guessing he ratted them out to the club to save his ass. But that was when he left for New Mexico. He had a group of women and girls that he was working on at the time as well as my mom and me. He took us all with him. I think he had some grand plan to become this big shot in human trafficking, but the cartels already have that territory covered. The cartel took all but three of us. Me, Mom and one other woman, Lucy."

My voice cracked saying her name. I missed her almost as much as I missed my Mom. Cujo's palm slid up and down my thigh and I lowered my hands to lift his between them, running my fingers over the calluses and scars that marred his skin. While keeping my gaze locked on our hands, I kept talking.

"We headed north to Vegas. I was three years old. He pimped out Mom and Lucy so that meant I spent a lot of time with him. He mostly sat me in front of a TV or locked me out in the yard. It was one of those days that I was outside that I shifted for the first time." Another shudder ran down my spine. "I was climbing this huge tree, way higher than I should have. I slipped and fell. My ocelot rose up and took over. In my feline form, I landed safely on the grass, unharmed. But Kevin must have been watching because within seconds he was there, splashing this horrible smelling liquid over me. It forced me back to my human form and before I could catch my breath, he slapped the bracelets on." I shook my head, trying to remove the memories of that day. "We'd been in Vegas about two years when Lucy died. Guess the downside to controlling people with drugs is the risk that they'll use them to end their life." I shrugged and pulling one hand free of his, dashed the tears from my cheeks. "With her gone, he started pimping me out." His hand curled around mine tighter, and I glanced over to see he'd gripped the steering wheel so tightly with the other, his knuckles were white. Realizing he was close to losing his shit again, I rushed to finish. "It was ten years later when Mom died. Same as Lucy, she overdosed. After that, Kevin moved us to Timber Cove. I looked older than I was, and he'd gotten false paperwork before we left Vegas and used that to prove I was an adult when he put me to work in the new area. We lived outside of Timber Cove, and he'd cycle me through several towns around the area. You know the rest."

Silence filled the cab as I waited for his response. I dashed more tears as I took a shaky inhale. He didn't take his hand from mine, which I took as a sign he wasn't totally disgusted by me now. When he rolled to a stop at a traffic light, I looked over at him to find he was staring at me.

"That motherfucking bastard will get what's coming to him. I promise you, he'll *never* lay another fucking hand on you again. You'll never have to sell your body to survive. That hell is over. You're mine and I'll always take care of you, make sure you have everything you need. You understand me?"

I nodded. "I hear you. It's just hard to believe, you know? After so long of having nothing good, I don't know how to accept this." I waved a hand between the two of us.

He leaned over and pressed a kiss to my lips before he had to focus back on driving as the light changed.

"I get it. I was locked up and experimented on for twenty-six years. So, yeah, I fucking get it. But we're both free now and I vow to you, we're gonna enjoy it. Somehow, we'll learn how to live free and we'll have a good life."

Tears ran down my cheeks again, but this time they were of happiness. Of hope. Because I wanted desperately to believe my mate's words, but until I knew Kevin was dead, I couldn't believe my freedom would last.

· · · · · · · · · ·

Daniela

I paced the shadows of the parking lot outside the Iron Hammers MC clubhouse while I waited. I could go inside. I was welcome to, but if I went inside, I'd get drawn into conversations and if I lost track of time, I might miss the arrival of the newest club members. It was vital I catch them before Joaquin attempted to get them inside.

The two prospects guarding the gate kept glancing my way, I made them nervous. I had that effect on most people, human and supernatural alike. Many believed I painted my face and neck, but I didn't. The markings that covered patches of my skin all over my body were the markings of my kind. We were born with them and in times gone by, we'd had to cover up with either clothing and masks or heavy makeup in order to venture out into society.

The Iron Hammers MC, with all their various shifters, were more understanding than most and I could show them my face without fear of what they'd do to me. After all, it had been this club that had rescued me four years ago and brought me here to the safety of Galveston. While I made them nervous, it wasn't the way that most of my face except for around my left eye was marked with black and white to look like a skull, the way a neon blue-green shimmered around my right eye that caused it. Nope, it was my ability to see into the past and the future that had these men on their toes. Which I understood completely. No one liked others knowing their deepest secrets. Most of the time I didn't like knowing them, but my talent wasn't something I could turn on and off with a switch. It came when it pleased, gifting me with often unwanted snippets of the nightmares those around me have lived through. Although, even if I did have a switch to turn them off, I wouldn't. Together with this club of Viking bikers, my visions had led to many humans and shifters being saved from traffickers and abuse. It was an honorable use for my skills, something I was proud to help with.

But the Iron Hammers MC hadn't always been this beacon of light. Before Joaquin and his kin came to clean the place out, the club had been neck-deep in trafficking. They gathered women and girls whenever they could, getting them hooked on drugs and using their bodies before selling them to an even worse fate. It was that past that had me pacing this parking lot.

I'd had several visions about Lily-Rose and her mate, Cujo, over the past month. It was the reason I'd sent Joaquin with a team over to northern California last week. Both shifters had suffered so much trauma in their short lives, they deserved to have some love and peace now and I knew Galveston was the right place for them. The Iron Hammers would be better with Cujo among them, too. His skills would be a welcome addition to the raids they went on to save others.

My thoughts were cut short when the sound of Harleys filled the air. I slid deeper into the shadows of the building as the bikes rolled through the gate followed by a sleek, black SUV. Once all the vehicles were shut off, I stepped out into the light and Joaquin turned to me.

"You come with good or bad news?"

I smiled up at the big Alpha. "I've come to welcome the newest additions to our pack."

He grunted, knowing me well enough to know there was more to it, but also knowing I wouldn't reveal a damn thing before I was ready to.

"Well, let's get you introduced then."

With a nod, I followed behind him over to the SUV where Cujo was helping his mate out of the vehicle. She was a petite little thing. Long, blonde hair and slender curves that made me think of a doll. My heart warmed at the care Cujo was taking with her, the mate-bond already shining bright between the two. Lily-Rose was still fragile and didn't yet trust her newfound freedom, but I knew in time she would. Cujo would guard and protect her while she stretched her wings and blossomed into the woman she was always destined to be.

But first, she'd need a little of my help.

Chapter Nine

Cujo

I didn't dare ask her anything else as we continued our drive to the clubhouse. I was barely keeping my fury under wraps at it was. If she told me any more of the hell she'd lived through, I was likely to completely lose it and turn wolf. I knew that just like she didn't fully believe Joaquin, she didn't fully trust my word yet either. But I'd show her. She would always be protected from here on out.

We followed the bikes into the yard of the clubhouse. The fear and tension radiating off Lily-Rose increased ten-fold when the gate rolled shut behind us. I needed both hands to get my rig parked, but as soon as I had things sorted, I reached over to retake her hand in mine.

"It's okay, sweetheart. You're safe. I'll protect you."

She looked into my eyes and the fear in her gaze gutted me. I never wanted to see that look in her steel-blue irises again.

"Okay."

At her whispered word, I released her and got out, rushing around to her side to be there before she could exit on her own. I was helping her down when I sensed someone approaching. On alert, I turned and moved to stand in front of her at the same time. With her anxiety and fear so high, my wolf was on high alert, needing to take care of whatever it was scaring our mate.

Joaquin held his palms up. "Whoa, Cujo. Fuck, you need to settle the fuck down already. You're both safe here on club property. No one gets through those gates we don't invite."

But it wasn't Joaquin I'd sensed, it was the woman standing beside him. She'd attract attention anywhere she went with her face like it was. She'd painted herself to look like she was wearing a skull mask, one that was broken to reveal the skin of her left temple around her eye and part of her cheek. It was all black and white except for around her right eye, tip of her chin and center of her right cheek that had a neon blue-green shimmer mixed in. Her unpainted skin was bronzed that together with the face paint, had me thinking this was Daniela. Well, that and she radiated a power and magic that would have had even me contemplating running if Joaquin hadn't assured us she was friendly.

"That Daniela?"

Joaquin nodded at my question and stepped aside so she was revealed fully to me. She wore a long black dress that was loose and flowed around her as though there was a stiff breeze, which there wasn't. She was one spooky female.

"May I meet your mate, wolf?"

Her voice was soft and heavily accented, but still easily understood. I reached behind me and moved Lily-Rose in front of me. Unsure what Daniela had planned, I wrapped my arm around her waist to keep my mate close. She didn't fight my hold at all. In fact, she leaned against me.

Daniela smiled at Lily-Rose and in the evening light, it was creepy as fuck. That face paint of hers really was a great mind-fuck.

"It is nice to meet you, Lily-Rose. You, too, Cujo. I am Daniela Nunes Souza and I'm here to show you to your new home."

Joaquin jerked his head toward the woman. "What the fuck? They're staying here at the clubhouse until we get her father dealt with."

With absolutely no fear, something I had to respect, Daniela faced off against Joaquin with a raised eyebrow. "You try to lock them down inside that building, Lily-Rose will escape and run. Sledge took her mother and held her within those walls while he negotiated with Kevin. Even if Lily-Rose's fear didn't prevent her from being comfortable here, her father knows the layout of this building. For them, at this time, the clubhouse is not safe. I have found a place close to my home near the San Luis Pass." She turned back toward us, focusing her gaze on my mate. "It backs onto an area of swamp. There's not much coverage during the day, but you'll be able to roam freely at night." She frowned, flicking her glare my way a moment. "But no chasing or hunting snakes. They are off limits."

This had to be the most bizarre conversation of my life.

Feeling like she required a response, I spoke, "No hunting snakes. Got it."

Stiffening, Lily-Rose pulled away from me and I loosened my hold but didn't release her completely. I wasn't sure what she was thinking but hoped she wasn't going to fucking attack this woman. As much as I could withstand spells and magic, I wasn't sure I could hold off someone of her power.

"How do you know what happened to my mother?"

She bowed her head slightly at Lily-Rose's growled question. "I'm sorry I didn't explain myself. You have no need to fear me. I am not now, nor have I ever been involved with your father or Sledge and his minions. I am a rainbow boa shifter, a natural born magic user. My abilities include visions. Some of the future, some of the past. It was thanks to a vision that I sent Joaquin and his men to California to aide you. I mean you and your mate no harm."

No matter how powerful this woman was, she wasn't the Alpha. It was Joaquin who I had to obey now, no one else. Well, aside from my mate. I caught his gaze. "What do you say to this? As Alpha."

He looked from Daniela to Lily-Rose, then to me. "I learned some time ago not to go against her advice. You can trust that anything she tells you is the truth. Those visions of hers never fail us." He held his finger up in the air. "But before you go, I'd like you both to come inside, meet everyone. I've got a few things to give you. And I'll be sending a few brothers to keep watch over your cabin. Until Kevin is dealt with, I'm not taking any chances."

· · · · · · · · · ·

Lily-Rose

I struggled to tear my attention away from Daniela as Cujo guided me over toward the main door. She was stunning, even with the strange face paint that now I was closer, I wasn't so sure was paint. Could they be natural markings of her kind? Either way, it didn't detract from her beauty. Long, thick black hair, dark eyes that looked clear into your soul. She wore a gorgeous, long dress that I'd thought was black, but now we were in more light I could see it was a dark red. She moved so smoothly, I honestly wasn't sure if she was walking or floating.

The moment we passed inside, I forced my gaze from her and around the room. Clearly, at some point long ago this had been a grand old house. The sweeping staircase that led upstairs was stunning and looked freshly restored.

Chaos came and stood beside me. "They came up great, huh? We have a brother that's real good with wood and building shit."

I nodded as I let my gaze continue around the large room we were in. I guessed it may have been some sort of ballroom or something originally, but now it looked like a club or bar... but with a mix of couches and tables with chairs. Some of the walls had drywall showing, as though they were currently renovating.

"The last guys left us one hell of a mess. Even before we came in and made it worse. We're slowly getting it all fixed up." With a wink, Chaos moved off toward the bar calling out for a beer on his way.

Joaquin took his place beside us. "C'mon, we'll head to my office."

Cujo's palm was on my lower back and he guided me along after Joaquin. I could feel eyes on me but I didn't feel threatening energy coming from any of them, so I did my best to stay calm. I was beyond grateful that Daniela had thought to find us somewhere to stay away from here, though. As much as I was holding it together for now, I was quite sure I wouldn't have been able to keep it together all night.

Joaquin nodded toward a couch. "Take a seat, this won't take long."

Cujo sat first, tugging me until I sat across his lap. Wrapping his arms around me, he tucked me in against his chest. His warmth instantly surrounded me, easing all my nervousness. With a sigh, I snuggled in as he began to play with my hair.

"You two are fucking nauseating with that shit. Right, so here's a cut for you to wear, Cujo. I'll order your name patch and shit to add to it. And we'll get Lily-Rose's old lady cut sorted too. The deal is, you're a prospect for a year before we'll vote on you becoming a full brother. Unlike some other clubs, we don't treat our prospects like dirt. You have skills we need, and I expect you'll willingly use them for us."

Cujo grunted in response and I stayed right where I was.

"As your Alpha, I can reach out to you telepathically. As Cujo has already experienced, I can also draw away pain and other emotions, so if either of you get into trouble, you reach out to me." He waited for us both to nod. "The pack and club are basically the same, although we do have a few humans in the club that aren't technically part of the pack. Even though it's been four years, we still come up against some bullshit from other clubs who had run-ins with the old guard. It doesn't happen often thankfully, but it does happen. We took over down here with the blessing of the Satan's Cowboys MC. Together with the Charon MC, they helped us clean the old guard out so both those clubs are allies and if you see their colors, you can be sure they'll have your backs."

I'd never heard of either of those clubs and wasn't sure how I felt about being surrounded by so many men. "How often will we see those other clubs? Are they shifters too?"

Joaquin shook his head. "As far as I'm aware, both clubs are fully human. The Satan's Cowboys MC control a lot of Texas, so we come under their jurisdiction. Basically, we exist because they allow it. So, we pay our dues to them and occasionally do runs for them. Not often, thankfully. Only time we go anywhere near drugs is when we do those jobs. The Charon MC is in Bridgewater, which is about an hour northeast from here. We've helped them out a few times over the years and they us. They're a little bigger than us, all good, solid men. Scout is their president and he can be trusted to take care of you. Like us, they run a clean club, no drugs. Once you get settled in, we'll arrange a run and barbecue so you can meet them and all their women and kids."

I frowned. Women and kids? "So, these clubs are like a big family?"

Joaquin smiled warmly. "Exactly. Most MCs function like a big 'ol family. It's not always smooth sailing, but you can fucking count on them to take your back. You're both part of this pack and MC now, and we'll help you deal with Kevin and any other shit that might come your way. And you'll both return the favor, yeah?"

He raised an eyebrow at me, waiting for a response.

"Not sure what use I'd be, but of course I'd protect my family."

Cujo's deep voice vibrated his chest beneath me, "You know I'll honor my word. I said I'd accept you as my Alpha, so this is my pack too now."

Joaquin leaned back against his desk, arms folded over his chest. "Excellent. No fucking clue where Daniela is taking you, but I'm guessing it'll be close to her place. She lives out of town, down the coast a way. Your ocelot will love it, Lily-Rose, and it's far enough away from the town that your wolf shouldn't lose his shit, Cujo. I wasn't joking about sending out guards. I'll have at least three brothers out there at all times to keep watch so don't go hunting any animals, yeah?"

Cujo laughed as he stood and set me on my feet.

"Sure, boss. No hunting till we know who we're eating. Got it."

That had me grinning. I didn't imagine it would be a good start if we took out some of our new pack by accident.

Chapter Ten

Cujo

Thankfully, it didn't take long to drive south down to the house Daniela had found us. I was a little nervous over what sort of dwelling it would turn out to be, had imagined it would be some sort of falling down piece of shit cabin out in a swamp. It was a pleasant surprise when we headed into a new looking estate. My wolf allowed me to see clear enough in the night to notice there were very few houses. When Daniela guided us to park in front of a large, modern stilt house, I was happy to see it had a closed in garage beneath.

"The current owner is a friend. I keep an eye on this place for him. He rents it out as a holiday rental, so it's fully furnished. If you like it, I'm sure he can be convinced to sell it to you."

Getting out of the SUV, I moved around to the passenger side, but didn't open Lily-Rose's door until the three bikes that had followed us from the clubhouse had parked and the men had shifted and taken off into the marsh land behind the house. I looked up and down the street to make sure no one else was around before I opened the door and helped Lily-Rose down. With a gentle smile that melted some of the ice off my mood, she put her hand in mine and we followed Daniela up the sturdy timber stairs.

My mind returned to protection mode as we came to the wrap around porch on the main level. "These stairs the only way to the upper level?"

Daniela gave me a nod as she pulled a key out to unlock the door to the interior. "Yes, any human visitors you get will need to come up this way. But some breeds of shifter won't need the stairs to get up here."

Like her snake form. But shifters weren't my concern at the moment. Lily-Rose's human father was, so only having one point of entry to worry about was a good thing. Lily-Rose and I would both be able to safely jump down over the porch railing if we needed to, so we'd have multiple escape routes while Kevin would need to use the stairs to both gain entry and to exit.

Before going inside, I ran my gaze over the marsh at the rear of the property, seeing the glint of animal eyes as my new packmates roamed the area eased my worry and once the door was open, I followed the women inside.

"You both stay put. Let me check there's no one else in here."

Daniela rolled her eyes and Lily-Rose shook her head with a smirk, but they both stayed put while I took off to do a quick search. It thankfully didn't take long to discover we were indeed alone in the house and I returned to the women to find them chatting quietly to one another. Daniela was smiling at my mate as though she were enjoying their discussion. That made me smile. Lily-Rose was already making friends, not that I doubted she would. My mate was a ray of sunshine few would be able to resist wanting to be close to.

She looked up as I came to stand behind Lily-Rose, wrapping my arm around her waist to pull her back against me.

"All good?" She waited for my nod before continuing, "I was just telling your mate how my house is down the road a little. We're technically neighbors, for the moment. If you need anything, feel free to drop in or call me." She handed Lily-Rose a slip of paper, presumably with her number on it. "I'll leave you both to settle in. Kevin won't find you tonight."

Before I could ask about if she knew when Kevin would find us, she passed me a key then turned and headed for the door. Following, I held the way open for her. She seemed to disappear into the darkness. Even with shifter sight, I couldn't see her.

With a shake of my head, I shut things up, flipping the lock. "That's one strange lady."

Lily-Rose folded her arms over her chest as she leaned against the kitchen counter. "I think she's nice. Her talents are amazing. She's offered to help me train to use my abilities so I can better protect myself."

A growl broke free before I could stop it. "It's my job to protect you."

I moved to stand in front of her, resting my palms on her hips as she looked up at me with a frown.

"You can't be by my side twenty-four-seven, Cujo. I need to be able to fend for myself. I refuse to be a spectator in my own life anymore." She reached up to cup my face between her palms, her touch instantly calming my wolf. "I promise if you're around I'll let you do the protecting. I just want to be able to save myself if, for some reason you're not able to. You can understand that, can't you?"

Closing my eyes, I took a deep breath. She was right. I couldn't always be with her, not long-term. Leaning down, I pressed my lips to hers, briefly kissing her before lifting back up to look into her eyes.

"I get it, I do. And I want you to always be safe. I'd just prefer to be the one who makes that fucking happen."

Slipping her hands down to my chest, she grinned up at me. "You wanna be the big, bad wolf who comes in to rescue the damsel in distress, huh?"

Her touch seared through me. That, together with having her scent surrounding me, had my cock throbbing with need, making it difficult to focus on our conversation.

"Somethin' like that."

Her eyes darkened with desire and she leaned in, wriggling her hot little body against me. The friction over my hard dick had me growling as it upped my need to claim what was mine.

· · • • • • • · · ·

Lily-Rose

My mate was all raw sexuality when he got riled up like he was right now, and in response, my body lit up like a damn Christmas tree. I'd had every kind of sex there was more times than I could count, but no one had ever made me feel even half of what Cujo did.

Sliding my hands down his front, I kept going until I could grip the bottom of his t-shirt. Without taking my gaze from his, I started shoving the fabric up, running my fingers over every dip and bump of his muscles along with all the scars. With another of his sexy growls, he reached a hand over his head and pulled his shirt off, the fabric ripping in his haste.

We'd been so rushed in the hotel room, now I wanted to take a little more time. Learn his body. Looking over the flesh he'd revealed, my gaze caught on a particularly nasty looking scar and without thought, I moved to trace a fingertip over it. What he must have suffered to have so many scars... He gently wrapped his hand around mine, my gaze jerking up to his face as he lifted my hand to press a kiss against my palm.

"I'll tell you any damn thing you wanna know later, babe. Right now, I need to fuck you more than I need to breathe."

His crude words pushed a wave of heat through me, and I leaned in to press a kiss over his heart as I slid against him, making sure to rub against the rock-hard erection.

With another growl, he wrapped his hands around my hips, and I squealed as he easily lifted me and tossed me over his shoulder. He gave my butt a tap as he headed out of the living area, making me squeal again. With a rumbly chuckle, he then ran his hand up my thigh, under the skirt of the dress I was wearing. The feel of his rough, callused hands stroking over the sensitized skin of my thighs and butt had my arousal soaring. By the time he tossed me onto the mattress, I was desperate for him. For only the second time in my entire life I actually *wanted* sex. I stilled as that thought really sank in. Never had I imagined a situation in which I would crave anything sexual that I'd learned to hate. Tears stung my eyes as I marveled over how differently I looked at intimacy now. How could my mindset change so much in such a short time?

"Mate bond."

My ocelot seemed to think that was the answer to everything lately.

I gasped when Cujo took hold of my ankle and pulled me toward him until he could help me stand. The moment I was upright, he laid his lips over mine. He held nothing back, devouring my mouth in a way that had all thoughts fleeing my mind. All I could focus on was getting closer to my mate.

He broke the kiss and ran his gaze over my face.

"That's better. Need your focus here with me, not wherever the fuck you went earlier. Now, if you wanna keep these clothes, you need to strip. If I do it, I'm gonna tear everything off you."

With a contented sigh, I shivered at his growled words. Then reached for the hem of my dress to lift it up and over my head. One day I'd tease him with a slow striptease, but not today. Our mating in the hotel room had been rushed and over way too quickly, but now we had all night to touch and learn each other.

I couldn't wait to start.

Within seconds I was naked and when I looked back to Cujo, he was the same. Another shiver ran through me as I ran my gaze over him. He was perfectly imperfect. While he didn't have an ounce of fat on his lean, muscular frame, his skin was covered with scars. He'd covered up some of them with tattoos, but my shifter sight allowed me to see what he'd hidden beneath the ink. One day I'd be brave enough to ask him about what he'd been through, but that wasn't going to be tonight. Tonight was about the start of our future, not either of our pasts.

With a cheeky smile I moved close, pressing myself fully against his body, loving how the coarse hairs on his chest and torso felt against my skin and the way his erection pressed against the softness of my tummy. His ice-blue irises heated as he watched me. He didn't move to stop me or control my movements, as though he wanted to see what I'd do before he took over.

I'd never wanted to touch any of the men I'd been with previously. I'd always been all about getting them off as fast as I could so I could leave. But with Cujo, all I wanted to do was touch and caress. To learn every inch of his muscular body. My ocelot was purring with her contentment to be playing with our mate.

Slipping around him, I moved to his back, pressing kisses and running my palms over the wide expanse of muscles, inhaling his scent while leaving some of my own behind, marking him. This man was mine and I wanted the world to know it.

Chapter Eleven

Cujo

Lily-Rose had to be the most affectionate woman I'd ever met. I hated to think how suffocated she must have felt living the life her father had forced upon her. I was going to have to learn to be more attentive. I didn't think that'd be much of an issue, though. It was easy to reciprocate her attentions, which was a shock to me. Not only did her rubbing all over me as though she was in her feline form not bother me, but I actually fucking enjoyed it. Those fucking scientists that held me had made sure I related touch to pain, and by the time I got free, I never wanted to be touched by another human ever again. I'd always done everything I could to avoid it, but with Lily-Rose, I craved it. I needed to touch and be touched by her.

"Because she is our mate. Ours to protect and cherish."

I mentally gave my wolf a nod. It was going to be interesting with me and Lily-Rose learning how to be mates. Neither of us had grown up with parents or a pack to teach us anything about how mate bonds worked.

When she moved over to my other side, I lifted my arm so she could slip around to my front without having to break contact. She was so much shorter than me, she only had to duck a little to get under my arm. When she moved in front of me again and my cock was once more pressed against her soft tummy, I groaned as a spike of arousal went through me.

"You done playing, kitty?"

With a cheeky smile and glint in her eye, she leaned in. Curious at what she was planning, I stayed still to let her have her fun. That was, until she nipped at my nipple. Then, with a hiss, I jerked back in reflex. She wanted a little roughness, did she? I could give her that.

With a growl, I picked her up and tossed her onto the mattress. With wide eyes she looked up at me, like she hadn't expected me to do what I did. I paused, worried I'd scared her. I was about to apologize when her face broke out into a cheeky grin again and she started to slowly spread her legs, teasing me with what I wanted.

Pressing a knee on the mattress, I ran my palms up her legs, loving the way she shivered as I pushed them out far enough to give me the room I needed.

"My turn to play now, babe. And I distinctly remember promising you I'd take all night with you when I got the chance."

Before she could say a word, I lowered down and took a lick up her center, getting my first taste of her for the night. She groaned and lifted her hips up when I pulled back, making me laugh as I gripped her hips to hold her still while I buried my face back against her and got serious about making a meal out of my woman.

Her honeysuckle scent filled my senses as I continued to lick, nip and tease her pussy with my mouth. With a hum that had her gasping and tangling her fingers in my hair, I added two fingers to the mix, finger-fucking her as I tormented her clit.

"Cujo."

Her voice was barely more than a moan as she began to thrash on the bed. With one last swirl of my tongue around her clit, I lifted my face up to stare into her blissed-out countenance. I kept my fingers moving, loving the way she was squirming for me. As I found her g-spot within her core, I ground the heel of my palm against her clit, knowing it would send her flying. Her breath grew choppy as she grabbed fistfuls of the sheets.

"Come for me, my mate."

As if she'd been waiting on my words, she screamed and climaxed. Her core tightened around my fingers as I slid them free. Lowering my mouth back to her, I lapped up her cream and kept at her with slow, lazy strokes until she started to come down from her high. When she relaxed against the mattress, I moved up, pressing a kiss to the top of her bare mound before I continued my way up her body. I stopped when I got to her beautiful tits, sucking and biting each nipple while I tweaked and tugged on the other with my fingers.

I didn't ease my attention until she was once again squirming beneath me. I fully intended to wring so many orgasms from my woman that by morning she wouldn't know what day of the week it was, and maybe even forget her own damn name.

Continuing up her body, I took her mouth with mine, giving her a powerful, dominant kiss that let her know I was done playing and she was all fucking mine now. She wrapped her legs around my waist, digging her heels into my ass until I thrust forward and sunk balls deep inside her.

"Fuck, Lily-Rose... so fucking good."

"Mmm hmmm."

I would have chuckled at her moaned response, but I was too focused on how good it felt to her pussy squeezing the hell out of my cock on each thrust into her wet heat. I knew without a doubt that

I was never gonna get tired of fucking my mate. My woman.

· · • • • • • • · ·

Lily-Rose

The next morning, I woke to find my body was still blissfully sore in places. Never had I thought I'd be smiling after a night filled with so much sex, but here I was, unable to wipe the grin off my face. In my sleep, I'd rolled out of his reach, probably because the man was a damn furnace and I'd gotten overheated. Careful so I didn't wake my sleeping mate, I moved around so I could run my gaze over him. He lay on his back, his face toward me as he peacefully slept. He was so much larger than me, so much stronger. The sheets had slipped down to around his waist revealing his upper body, which was nothing but a whole lot of sexy muscles covered with various tattoos and scars.

Licking my lips, I ran my gaze over each one. One day I'd kiss each mark on his body, trace his tattoos with my tongue... I couldn't wait. But this morning, I had another idea that had my body growing damp in anticipation. I reached out and slowly moved the sheet until his entire body was revealed to me in the morning sunlight that crept in around the curtains.

Even flaccid, his dick was big. Not wanting him to wake yet, I bit back the moan that wanted to escape my throat as my body clenched and trembled in memory of exactly how good Cujo was at using that part of his anatomy. But for all the ways he'd taken me overnight, I'd still not been able to get a taste of him. That was about to change.

I'd been forced to learn early on how to be good at blow jobs, but I'd never once enjoyed it or looked forward to it. It was surreal to now be slowly crawling over the bed toward a man, being careful to not wake him and risk him stopping me from getting a taste of him. My mouth was watering by the time I was leaning over him close enough to be surrounded by his delicious pine and sea spray scent.

Barely resisting the urge to giggle at how much fun I was having sneaking up on my mate, I lowered and took the entirety of his dick in my mouth. Instantly, it began to harden and with a groan, he buried a hand in my hair.

"Fuck, Lily-Rose... feels so good."

Now he was awake, I moved to straddle his leg, rubbing my pussy against him as I took his now hard length as deep as I could. Swallowing against him when he hit my throat, he barked out a curse and shuddered. With a hum, I rose up his shaft, teasing my tongue around the rim before sucking on just the tip for a few moments.

His grip in my hair tightened when I brought my other hand into the mix, cupping his balls before gently rolling them. Within minutes, I had him bucking and squirming beneath me, mindless in the pleasure I was giving him. My heart soared that I could do this to my mate. He was so much physically stronger than I was, yet with just my mouth and hands on him for a few minutes, he was putty and at my mercy.

Pulling all the way off, I inched down a little so I could take his balls in my mouth. Gently sucking and tonguing him until he was cursing, I moved to lick up the underside of his cock before taking him back in deep, all the way to the back of my throat.

I continued to play, trying different things to learn exactly what would drive my mate wild. When I got my next taste of his pre-cum, I couldn't hold in my happiness. Purring, I went back to my ministrations.

"Fuck. I'm gonna come. Pull off if you don't wanna bellyful of me, babe."

I stilled until he looked down at me. The moment our gazes locked, I slid his length back inside my mouth, swirling my tongue around him until I couldn't, then humming until his cockhead tapped the back of my throat. When I swallowed against him, he barked out another curse and his dick throbbed against my tongue. I pulled back a fraction as he began to come so I could swallow every drop down. I didn't want to waste a drop, he tasted that good.

I was gently lapping at his still hard erection to clean him completely when, with a growl, he slipped his hands under my arms and pulled me up his body. My legs fell to either side of his torso. With a huge grin, I pressed my palms against his shoulders to lift up so I could look down into his face. My hair fell forward, forming a curtain around us as I moved to lay my lips against his.

When a growl rose from his mouth, I purred in response, loving that even after coming he was still hard and wanting more of me. Ending the kiss, I rubbed my nose up against his.

"Need to fuck you. How sore are you?"

His voice was full of gravel and it sent a shiver down my spine. I slid down a little, rubbing my aching sex over his abs while I nipped my way along his jaw before I responded.

"Not sore enough to stop me from wanting more of my mate."

Within seconds, his grip shifted from my ribs to my hips and he jerked me down, straight onto his erection. His hard length filled me completely and I arched up as I cried out his name. He sat up and nuzzled into my neck. I wrapped my arms around his neck while I shivered when he licked over his claiming mark.

Never in my wildest dreams had I ever believed I'd feel this good in the arms of a man. But I truly did. His arms around me, holding me tightly against him didn't feel confining or cruel in any way. All I felt was protected and safe. Loved, even.

I blinked back tears as I moved over him, the rise of emotions within me too much to contain. I'd never been so happy.

Chapter Twelve

Two days later

Cujo

As soon as I drifted off to sleep with Lily-Rose tucked in against me after I'd done her right, the oily darkness flowed over me and I knew I was in trouble. But sleep had me in its clutches and I couldn't break free until it was done with me. I should have known things were going too well with Lily-Rose to last. And it had nothing to do with her piece of shit father. After I'd first escaped from that fucking laboratory, I had nightmares every night. I'd lived on a knife's edge, trying anything I could to stay awake until I was so strung out, I'd start seeing my nightmares during the daylight hours.

Even after I'd fallen in with a street gang and learned what I needed to know to take care of myself, the nightmares still plagued my sleep. Until the first time I killed a man. Getting that fucker's blood on my hands stopped the nightmares for a while.

That's where my nightmare started tonight, the night of that first kill. I hadn't been in the gang long when one night I stumbled upon a man dragging a teenage girl into an alley. The girl was done up for a night out and I'd had no clue what the fuck she was doing in that part of town, but she was in trouble and needed help. I knew if I didn't step in to help the girl, no one would. If anything, those that saw what was going on would wait for the asshole to finish with her so they could take a turn.

I knew what it felt like to be taken against your will. There had been both male and female lab techs who'd taken great delight in fucking the beast. Those memories rose up and before I realized what I was doing, I was jogging down the alley behind the struggling girl. My fur had rippled over my skin, but I managed to push it down. I couldn't risk humans seeing me. Even those that inhabited the darkest corners of alleys would no doubt know what they could get for a lone shifter on the black market.

Pulling a switchblade from my pocket, I flicked it open as I approached. The girl was making enough noise her attacker had no idea he wasn't alone with his victim until I was on him. Yanking his hair back, I stabbed the knife into his neck, aiming for the vein just above his pulse. Blood spurted and he released the girl to grab at his neck as though he could put the blood back in somehow.

I kicked his body aside and turned to the girl. She sat on her ass in the dirt, her wide, shocked eyes on the rapidly dying man. I stepped between her and him and with a gulp, she slowly moved her gaze up to mine.

"P-please don't hurt me."

I shook my head. Like I'd kill a man to get to her? She wasn't that special. I held the palm not holding the knife out to her.

"Come with me. Others will attack if you stay here."

She hesitated a moment, her gaze going to the dark corners of the alley behind me. I knew the others were creeping in. None would show their faces while I was still here and armed, but as soon as I was gone, they'd pounce to grab anything valuable from the now dead man.

Her hand trembled as she rested it in mine. As soon as it made contact, I yanked her up and began to drag her to the entrance. She silently trailed behind me until we got closer to the better part of town where the streetlights still glowed. Before we got that far, she pulled on my hand, trying to get free.

Stopping, I turned on her. "What?"

"Y-you k-killed that m-man..."

I growled in frustration. "Yeah? So what? If I hadn't, he'd have beaten and raped you, then left you in that alley for all the other perverted fuckers that live down there to do the same. You'd have been dead by morning, if you were lucky. You really wanna get into me for saving your ass?"

She was pale under her smeared makeup and shook like a leaf. Not that I cared. Hopefully, she was scared enough she wouldn't pull the same shit again.

"How far away do you live? I can take you a little further, but I ain't risking being seen covered in blood in public."

She rubbed her palms up and down her arms. "Not far. I can get home from here."

I frowned at her. Something was off. "Not sure I believe you, princess. What the fuck you doing down here in the first place? Surely your momma told you what this place is? Hell, even the homeless folks don't come near this fucking part of town."

I suspected she was here for the same reason I was, but she must have been fucking high before she got here for her to think she'd survive. When she stayed silent, I rubbed the back of my neck with my clean hand.

"You were looking for fucking drugs, weren't you? And let me guess—you don't want your folks to find out. Well, I didn't just do what I did for you to get in trouble again so I'm staying with you for now."

Black swirled around us and the girl vanished, but that was okay, I knew she'd gotten home safely. I'd been right about her folks. Her father was a politician and had been furious at what had nearly happened to his little girl. As a gesture of appreciation, he took me under his wing and gave me more skills and contacts that propelled me into being a mercenary.

But my nightmare wasn't done with me just yet. It threw me back further into the past. When the blackness cleared, I bucked and screamed in denial. I was back in the lab, strapped down to a table and buck-ass naked. The door opened and when I saw who it was, ice flowed through my veins.

"Been looking forward to this, beast. I have a new test for you to pass."

My heart started racing. This was the first time. I'd been fifteen fucking years old when this happened. When I'd woken up to find myself stripped and strapped down.

She moved to the tray of instruments and lifted a syringe, prepping it in my line of sight before with a grin, she jabbed it into the vein in my inner thigh and fire raced up and landed in my balls. With a groan, my cock grew hard and panic set in.

I pulled at my arms and legs, trying to bust free of the leather straps but they held.

"No! Don't you fucking touch me, bitch."

The words made no difference as she tossed the empty syringe aside and reached to stoke my cock with her palm. The sensation sent pleasure through me, but the disgust and fear that I'd felt that day quickly overtook that. Especially when the bitch lifted her skirt up, stripped out of her underwear then climbed up onto the platform I was strapped to, moving to straddle my hips.

"Nooo!"

· · · • • • • • · ·

Lily-Rose

I'd never slept as peacefully as I had since meeting Cujo. For the past two evenings, since we'd moved to this house, he'd take me to bed and make me come so many times I'd fall into a blissful, dreamless sleep. But I didn't stay that way tonight. The bed jostled a moment before Cujo's arm knocked into my shoulder. I was on my side facing away from him but quickly turned over to see what he was doing.

His eyes were squeezed tightly shut and his arms and legs flailed as though he were fighting to free himself from something.

"Cujo? Wake up, Cujo. You're safe now."

He didn't react to my words at all but started to groan as he bucked and sweat slicked his skin. Touching him would be a risky, but what else could I do? I looked toward the window and out into the marshland behind our house. How close were the Iron Hammer brothers who were guarding us tonight?

The whimper that came out of my big, tough mate broke my heart and I just couldn't leave him to suffer a moment longer. I reached out and wrapped my palm around his bicep, intending on shaking him awake.

When I made contact, he stilled completely for a second, before with a bone chilling growl, he turned on me, forcing me onto my back as he caged me beneath his big body. With his eyes still firmly closed, he bared his teeth and fur rippled over his skin before receding.

Desperate to reach him, I lifted my palms to either side of his face then cleared my throat so I could raise my voice louder.

"Cujo! Wake up! You're safe with your mate. The past can't hurt you anymore."

I wasn't a stranger to nightmares that felt so real you couldn't tell if it was a memory, a dream or real life. But Cujo was stronger than I'd ever been, so while I'd never hurt anyone during my nightmares, I was worried for the destruction he could cause if he didn't wake up soon.

With a gasp, I jerked my hands away when he snapped toward my right one with his scary as fuck wolf's teeth bared. His eyes flicked open, but they were dull and glazed over, as though he still wasn't seeing what was actually in front of him but whatever his nightmare was telling him.

When his gaze locked onto my throat, my heart ached. I wouldn't be able to wake him. Whatever demons were running around his mind were in control. With tears in my eyes, I called on my animal half and shifted to my much smaller ocelot's body then slipped out from under him and sprang from the bed before racing out the room, heading toward the front door while Cujo roared in protest behind me.

I skidded to a stop, panicking over how the fuck I was going to open the door when it swung open. Animal instincts had me laying my ears down and hissing until I saw it was Daniella motioning for me to come out.

"Hurry, Lily-Rose. You must run and hide."

I bounded past her and when I was on the top of the handrail, I glanced back to see she'd shut the door and was sprinting for the stairs. Seeing she was safely away, I leapt off the balcony. Hitting the ground running, I entered the marsh behind our house. I didn't stop running until I found a clump of shrubs that were big enough to hide me.

Slipping into my chosen hiding spot, I crouched low and looked back toward the house as a loud crash filled the night air. Cujo's wolf broke through the door, then putting his front paws on the railing, howled to the night. I held my breath wondering if he'd attempt the jump. He wasn't feline, but he was big and strong, so he might be able to make it without risking injury. When he jumped down and headed to the stairs, I blew out my breath and prayed Daniela had found safety.

I didn't dare move from my hiding spot as Cujo's dark wolf came stalking into the marsh. He'd no doubt sniff me out, but if I moved, he'd lock onto me even faster. I was still trying to work out what I could do when I heard a small snick sound to my left then his body jerked. He turned to look toward where I'd heard the sound then with a snarl and growl, he ran in that direction.

But he didn't make it. After a few steps he crashed to the ground with a whine. Panic flowed through me. Had he been shot? Who was out there? If the Iron Hammers were in wolf form, they wouldn't be carrying weapons. I ran my gaze over the area, wondering where they were. Surely, they would have heard Cujo and come to investigate.

Before I could locate any sign of them, movement caught my eye and I carefully moved to see who it was that had been out of my sight to the left. When my father stepped out into my view, it took everything in me to hold in the hiss my ocelot wanted to let out. With my ears back, I stayed close to the ground and stalked forward, making the most of him being solely locked onto Cujo. I took comfort in the fact I couldn't smell blood on the air. Hopefully he'd only tranqed my mate, not shot him.

He reached Cujo and kicked his body until he was sprawled out on his side.

"Big fucker, ain't you? Bet you've had fun with my daughter. Hope it was worth it, because now it's time to pay up. Gonna get big bucks for you and your buddies." He paused to look back toward the housing estate. "Gonna be a bitch to carry you all over to the truck..."

While he was lost in thought, planning how to load up his trophies, I crept closer, not stopping until I caught a glimpse of iridescent scales in the moonlight. I gave the large snake a nod, hoping like hell it was Daniela and not some exotic pet that'd escaped its owner.

"*Yes, it's me. You go for his throat, I'll contain the rest of him.*"

Damn, it was weird having someone else inside my head. I gave her another nod then focused up on my father's back as I prepared to pounce.

"*On three. One, two, three…*"

Before she'd finished speaking, I took off, leaping onto his back and quickly climbing up to wrap myself around the back of his neck. I caught sight of Daniela moving faster than a snake should be able to, wrapping herself around his arms and legs, holding him motionless and defenceless for me.

I looked up into his eyes, basking in the terror I saw for a moment before with a growl, I bared my teeth and tore into his throat. The coppery tang of blood filled my mouth, but I didn't stop. I tore chunks of flesh free, over and over again. I needed to be sure he couldn't come back. He'd threatened my mate. My ocelot wanted retribution for all the years he'd caged her and hurt me.

Chapter Thirteen

Cujo

"*Wake up, our mate needs us.*"

My wolf screaming inside my skull had me pushing the toxins through my system so I could wake up. Never thought I'd be grateful for anything that fucking lab had put me through, but the fact I could push drugs through my system quickly did come in handy.

Once I could break free from the drug's hold, I opened my eyes, shocked to find myself in wolf form, out in the marsh behind our house. Shifting to human, I stood on still shaky legs.

"What the fuck happened?"

Daniela stood beside me. "You had a nightmare, forcing your mate to flee for her life." She gestured a hand toward a cat gnawing on a body. "After following you both here, Lily-Rose's father was waiting for his chance."

I wasn't sure how the fuck she knew so much about everything, but decided to worry about that another time. "That's her father?"

She nodded. "What's left of him. Apparently, he'd really pissed off your mate's ocelot. That is a lot of pent-up rage."

I was struck mute in shock for a minute. My sweet, gentle mate was tearing her father apart. Blood, flesh and bones were getting tossed aside as she made her way down his body. The man was clearly dead and not coming back. I needed to stop this and get her back inside before the authorities were called in by someone. If I'd had a nightmare, I could only imagine the noise I'd made.

I took a step forward and stepped on a stick, purposefully making noise to get her attention. With her ears back flat, she turned to hiss and growl at me. Fuck, she was something else. So fierce and strong.

"Hey, my little kitty, you did good but it's over now. We need to get back inside and away from this mess before the cops come."

I held out my arms for her, but she backed away, digging her claws into her prey and dragging what was left of the bastard who'd abused her for most of her life with her.

"Think it through, Lily-Rose. The authorities arrive and see a cat tearing into a human, they're gonna shoot first, ask questions later."

But she wasn't listening. Her animal was ruling her thoughts and actions. I turned toward Daniela. "Can you help me out here?" She raised an eyebrow at me. "Please."

With a nod, she lifted a palm toward the ocelot who hissed and tried to run but couldn't seem to move. Then with a swirl of amber sparks, her naked human body crumpled to the bloody ground. I rushed forward and gathered her up against me. She trembled and mumbled something I couldn't make out.

"Shh, little kitty. I got you. It's gonna be all right."

Even with her chattering teeth, I made out what she said next. "Others. He hurt the others."

I turned to Daniela once more and she nodded. "I've already alerted Joaquin. He's on his way to collect them. All will be well. Take your mate back home, Cujo."

She reached out and gripped my bicep. I jerked against her hold when a shock of power shot up my arm, into my brain.

"What the fuck, woman?"

She patted my arm, ignoring my glare. "You can thank me later. No more nightmare rampages for you."

I paused for a moment longer, wondering whether to ask why she didn't pull that shit before tonight. A siren in the distance got me focused back on what was important. Magic users were notoriously difficult to make sense of, so I figured I'd leave it alone and just be grateful.

As fast as I could, I got us inside our home, wincing at the damage my wolf had done to the front door. I rushed through to the bathroom and sat Lily-Rose on the toilet.

"Don't move. I'll be right back."

Then I dashed back to the front door and lifted it from where it lay on the ground and did the best I could to get it back into the door frame. I ended up using a couple chairs to keep it upright. Hopefully, it'd be enough to have the cops not looking twice at it.

Moving back to the bathroom, I didn't bother turning on any lights. Both of us had excellent night vision so didn't need them, and they'd only attract the attention of the police.

Lily-Rose hadn't stayed where I'd left her, but I hadn't really expected her to. She was in the shower, head down as the water poured over her, washing the blood from her skin. When she'd shifted back to human, it had cleaned off any mess her ocelot had made, but she'd then fallen into the mess so had still been covered in blood. As was I from carrying her. Tossing my clothes into the corner, I moved into the shower stall.

"Hey, babe."

She raised her head and pressing her palms against my pecs, stared up into my face. The red rimming her eyes broke my heart.

"He's really gone?"

I ran my knuckles down her soft cheek. "Yeah, Lily-Rose, your kitty took care of him for good."

Slipping her hands lower then around my waist, she snuggled in against me. "Didn't like seeing him shoot you."

I shook my head on a chuckle. "Yeah, caught that. My fierce little protector."

Gently, I washed her body and hair, then gave myself a quick wash before flipping off the taps. As she allowed me to dry her off without complaint, I couldn't help but grin. My poor baby was tired as hell after the eventful night.

Once dry, I lifted her up and carried her back to our bed. She was already dozing when I settled her on the mattress and curled myself around her. I was the luckiest fucking wolf in existence. I knew there'd be questions tomorrow, and work to be done to clean up after tonight but for now we were safe, and I had my claimed mate in my arms.

What more could a feral shifter like me ask for?

· · • • • • • · ·

Lily-Rose

A loud bang jerked me from my sleep and had me reaching for Cujo, but his side of the bed was cold and empty. Blinking my eyes open, I sat up and looked around the room as my brain clicked into gear and I remembered what had happened last night.

Cujo's nightmare and subsequent rampage out into the marshland, my father tranqing him and me rushing to his aid. The memories flashing through my mind had me gagging. Scrambling from the bed, I skidded into the bathroom, throwing up into the toilet.

I'd killed my father. And not cleanly. My ocelot had torn him to shreds. Quite literally.

Tears stung my eyes as I retched into the toilet again, dry heaving now there was nothing left to bring up.

A large palm smoothed up my back before Cujo lifted my hair away from my face, holding it back for me. Once I was done, he leaned over and hit the flush button before he scooped me up off the floor and stood me between him and the sink.

"Rinse your mouth out, babe. Then I'll take you back to bed."

As I followed his instructions another series of loud bangs came from the back of the house. With a frown, I tried to turn to see past his big body. "What's going on out there?"

He lifted me up against his chest and headed out of the bathroom. "A couple of the brothers are helping me fix the door I busted last night."

I moved against him until I could wrap my arms around his neck. "It really happened, didn't it?"

He sat on the edge of the bed, his arms wrapping around my body, holding me to him firmly.

"Yeah, it really happened. I'm so fucking sorry, Lily-Rose. Daniela said I scared you into fleeing the safety of the house. I never wanted to scare you, or you to fear me."

His body shuddered and I tightened my grip, lifting myself up so I straddled his lap.

"I know you'd never hurt me intentionally, but you were trapped in your head. I tried to wake you…"

He buried his face in against my throat, pressing a kiss to his claiming mark. Ignoring the arousal that was flowing through me, I cleared my throat.

"What about Kevin's body? Did the police find it yet?"

He nodded against my neck before he lifted up to look into my eyes. "Yeah, they came while we were sleeping. There's tape and shit strung up out in the marsh. Horrible animal attack. The came by earlier to let us know to be careful until they could catch whatever animal it was. There's some traps and other crap out there that we'll need to be careful of for a while. I'm sure within a few weeks, they'll pack it all away and move on when there's no more attacks."

It was my turn to shudder. "I can't believe *I* did that."

He ran his knuckles down my cheek, and when I looked into his eyes, I saw the pride shining there.

"You were so fierce, my little kitty. Fucking love you can take care of business like that. Your ocelot had a debt to collect on your old man. Hopefully she's more settled this morning, having gotten her vengeance."

Knowing he wasn't judging me harshly for what I'd done, loosened my muscles and I relaxed in against him, slipping my hands down his shirt to the hem where I started to gather up the fabric.

"She's very content this morning, it was my human side that was horrified at the violence."

He pulled his shirt off over his head before responding, "Well, how about I make sure I'm always between you and danger in the future. I'll be the one to kill anyone who comes at you."

My ocelot raised her head and rumbled her disapproval, the sound slipping out my lips without my permission. Heat flared over my cheeks as Cujo laughed. "Guess she's not okay with that. I'm sure we'll find a compromise that allows her to go hunting on occasion. Oh, and Daniela dropped off an amulet for you to wear. So you can conjure up clothes after shifting." He paused to run his gaze down my naked body. "Fuck, Lily-Rose, I love you more than I thought I could ever love someone. You're simply perfect. My sweet warrior ocelot."

The heat in my cheeks grew and I knew I must be flushed bright red by now, but the way my heart swelled under his praise had me preening.

"And I love you, my rampaging protector. After everything I'd seen in my life, I didn't think men like you even existed. I'll never be able to thank you enough for saving me from that cell and showing me there's so much more to life."

With tears blurring my vision, I cupped his face and leaned in to press a kiss to his lips, with a growl he turned us so I was underneath him on the mattress. Since I'd slept naked, he had full access to every inch of me. Access he took full advantage of as his hands and mouth trailed from my lips down my body.

I arched my spine when he took his first lick up between my thighs. A happiness and joy I'd never felt before radiated out of me, making me grin as I lifted my hips against his touch, begging for more.

My ocelot preened within me before she whispered a secret I had to bite my lip to not call out. I'd tell Cujo later he was going to become a father, if I said something now, he'd stop what he was doing with his oh so talented tongue. Which would be criminal.

Running my fingers into his hair, I pulled him in closer as I got closer to a climax. Even past the arousal spiraling within me, a deep contentment settled over me. I'd found a future I'd never been brave enough to even dream of, and there was nothing I wouldn't do to keep it.

The End

More Iron Hammers MC stories will be coming soon!

Want to know more about Jaxson & Alina?

Check out Cyndi Faria's

"Jaxson's Blue Moon"

for their full story!

Blurb:

Alina Sloan

After a cruel packmaster claimed me as his property, I ran from him and landed in Deputy Jaxson Salvador's bed, a rival alpha wolf. Now, I don't know who my twins' father is. Not that it matters when I find myself kidnapped. There's only one wolf who can rescue me—assuming he'd even want to after what I did to him.

Jaxson Salvador

After Alina Sloan tore my heart out and left, I pushed the pain aside and focused on my job—working as a Deputy to keep my territory safe. But all my plans got tossed aside when I discovered Alina had been kidnapped by a shifter trafficking ring. Alina may still hate me, but I'm willing to set pride aside to protect my family, —even if going after the one who had her taken could destroy any chance I have at keeping her for myself.

Buy link:
www.books2read.com/jaxsonsbluemoon/

About The Author

Khloe Wren lives in rural South Australia with her husband, two daughters and an ever changing list of animals!

She started writing in 2013 and has published over 30 books since then in the romantic suspense genre. She writes both paranormal and contemporary stories, including her best selling series Charon MC.

Khloe enjoys writing outside of the box and she loves her heroes strong, and her heroines even stronger.

Other Books By Khloe

Charon MC:

Inking Eagle

Fighting Mac

Chasing Taz

Claiming Tiny

Chasing Scout

Tripping Nitro

Scout's Legacy

Mac's Destiny

Losing Bash

Finding Needles

Forging Blade

Taming Keys

Fire and Snow:

Guardian's Heart

Noble Guardian

Guardian's Shadow

Fierce Guardian

Necessary Alpha

Protective Instincts

Other Titles:

Fireworks

Scarred Perfection

Scandals: Zeck

FireStarter

Deception

Mine To Bear

Lightning Source UK Ltd.
Milton Keynes UK
UKHW020706251021
392801UK00009B/313